We Are Rich

We Are Rich

STORIES

DORI CARTER

Other Press

New York

Copyright © 2009 Dori Carter

Production Editor: Yvonne E. Cárdenas

Book design: Simon M. Sullivan

This book was set in 10.75 pt Times Roman by Alpha
Design & Composition of Pittsfield, NH.

10 9 8 7 6 5 4 3 2 1

LIBRARY OF CONGRESS CATALOGING-IN-PUBLICATION DATA

Carter, Dori.
We are rich : stories / Dori Carter.
p. cm.
ISBN 978-1-59051-307-1 (hardcover)—ISBN 978-1-59051-329-3 (e-book)
1. Wealth—Fiction. 2. Social status—Fiction. 3. Social
classes—Fiction. 4. Social mobility—Fiction. 5. Snobs
and snobbishness—Fiction. 6. City and town life—Fiction.
7. California—Fiction. I. Title.
PS3553.A774W43 2009   813'.54—dc22   2008038412

PUBLISHER'S NOTE:
This is a work of fiction. Names, characters, places, and
incidents either are the product of the author's imagination or
are used fictitiously, and any resemblance to actual persons,
living or dead, events, or locales is entirely coincidental.

For my dearest Suzanne and Ross,
with gratitude and all my love

Contents

We Are Rich

ALL ABOUT TOWN

by ALISTAIR TRIMBLE

Singing Sensation Mario Lanza Comes to Rancho Esperanza

"Only in Rancho Esperanza could you have Shakespeare, an aviator legend and the most beautiful girls in California all under one roof!" United States Marine Second Lieutenant Lincoln Crowell—all of nineteen years old—summed it up for everyone who was at Mrs. Cyrus Stevens' Casa de las Flores last night to bid summer adieu.

The always soignée Mrs. Stevens floated into her famed music pavilion dressed in a filmy Adrian creation made of white mousseline de soie with three tiers of ruffles at the floor-length hem. She then introduced a twenty-two-

year-old sensation she had recently heard sing at the Berkshire Music Festival. This darkly handsome tenor is named Mario Lanza and has been compared to the legendary Caruso. He performed selections that ranged from the impassioned tragic "I Pagliacci" to the charming and jolly comic opera "The Merry Wives of Windsor," for which he received a standing ovation.

Among the seventy guests who enjoyed the young Mr. Lanza was Mrs. Stevens' old friend, Charles Lindbergh, out from Detroit. He spoke briefly about his work as technical advisor to Henry Ford at the Willow Run plant, where the B-24 Liberator Bombers are being built. "I'm very impressed with the great job the women on the assembly line are doing," Lucky Lindy told all assembled. "Also, their high moral character—especially compared to the men." The ladies in attendance greeted this with much laughter, cheers and applause.

Her servants off doing their part for the war effort, Mrs. Stevens recruited daughters Hadley and Mercedes, along with friends Chicky Stokes and Delilah Porter, to pass out splendid refreshments. After the concert, guests strolled the lovely gardens to the main house where a dinner worthy of Windsor Castle was served. You're sure right, Lieutenant Crowell. Only in Rancho Esperanza!

The Cook's Boy
Peter Jorgensen

Dwight D. Eisenhower once said, "We were poor but the glory of it was we never knew it." Maybe in Abilene, Kansas, he couldn't figure it out, but in Rancho Esperanza, California, if your family didn't have money, no one ever let you forget it. I was nine years old when we moved there, and even though the Vietnam War raged nightly on our Magnavox, and a marching-fucking-drugged-out-rampaging youth was upending America (and all but annihilating the Wasp Establishment in the process), Rancho Esperanza remained a town where Old Money and social prominence went hand in glove. Among the rich, and even those of us who weren't, it was simply understood: pedigree was everything. Not only *your* pedigree, but your horses' and your dogs' as well. My mother, whose parents were humble Danish dairy farmers, took the opposite approach and firmly subscribed to the Scandinavian code of *jantelovan*—don't show off. Though I suspect this was less a family ethos than a realization that we couldn't anyway, so why bother trying.

Until my father's death, we lived thirty miles and another world away from Rancho Esperanza, in a small, picturesque town founded in the nineteenth century by Danes—many of whose descendents were devoted to keeping alive the Danish spirit and the colorful heritage of their native land. Not only were the streets named for famous Danes, and the stores and restaurants built in the style of a prosperous Danish hamlet, but gracing our corner park was also a reproduction of the Little Mermaid looking a little perplexed—the ocean being on the other side of the mountains. It was a village of Danish bakeries and friendly shoppes selling cuckoo clocks, decorative nutcrackers, Royal Copenhagen, Christmas ornaments, and an astonishing assortment of knick-knacks that could only be destined for garage sales. Somehow, this was enough to bring in tourists, who ambled down the streets snapping photos of cupolas, windmills, and flower boxes as if they were on a walking tour of Europe. The only visual glitch in this otherwise fastidious tableau were the Mexican workers in *bracero* straw hats, who came to town from neighboring ranches to sell eggs from the backs of their rusted-out trucks.

Among her fellow Danes, my mother was known for her good looks, her Christmas pickled herring, her meatballs in beer, and her *pandekager*. Another attractive young widow might have gotten a job in the local smorgasbord, donned a dirndl and lacy white apron, and set her sights on a new husband, but my mother was determined to never again be dependent on a man. Parlaying her limited culinary repertoire, she secured a position as cook to the most prominent family in Rancho Esperanza—Lincoln and Chicky Crowell. With congenital fortitude she sold or gave away most of our belongings, and we moved over the mountain and into the two-bedroom "gardener's cottage" on the Crowells' fifty-two acre estate—which had been left to Chicky by her parents, furniture and all.

As if to spite the cuddly moniker bestowed in childhood for her downy, flaxen hair, Chicky Crowell grew into a tough old bird whose imperiousness was completely natural, and whose effrontery was imbued with such High Wasp aplomb that she was able to carry it off with a complete and utter lack of pretense. As a child I found her intimidating. I was both anxious for her approval and eager to avoid being in her presence. She ruled her little fief by divine right, and being a lowly squire, I was expected to execute her decrees with alacrity.

"Would-you-*please*," she would say, pronouncing each and every word in that punctilious and commanding way she had of addressing inferiors, "*load* the picnic baskets *into* the trunk of the car and *do* be careful you *don't* allow-them-to-*tip*."

"Would-you-*take* the suitcases *down* from the bedroom and *place* them in-the-front-*hall*."

"I *need* this mailed *at* the post office as-*soon-as-possible*."

I don't think it ever occurred to Chicky Crowell to care what other people thought, least of all me. But who could blame her? Chicky's grandfather, Alfred Charles Stokes, had been a good, solid, Anglo-Saxon, Princeton-educated, Midwestern Republican banker who ran for governor of Ohio and—after he came to Bakersfield, California—ran a ten-thousand-acre cattle ranch on which oil was discovered. A. C. Stokes then moved his family from the dusty interior to the largest, most desirable ocean-view parcel in Rancho Esperanza. In our little town, Chicky Stokes Crowell was aristocracy as much as any Huntington, Stanford, or Crocker. Chicky's native sense of entitlement gave her an unquestioning faith in her own actions and opinions. The class distinction she so effortlessly conveyed offended my instinctive sense of justice, never more so than when she referred to me as "the cook's boy." In all the years we lived there, I was never sure if she thought it worth her while to remember my name was Peter.

Although I spent a great deal of time in the Crowells' house—known as the old Stokes estate—I never ventured out of the kitchen when the Crowells were in residence. I sat at the white enamel table doing homework or helping my mother grate cheddar cheese for the Welsh rarebit, a favorite of the Crowells' remarkably unremarkable palate. But when they were on vacation or gone for the day, the kitchen door was swung open and I gained entrée into a world of wealth I'd never imagined. Looking back, I feel sad for that young boy who was so fascinated by the most mundane, even utilitarian possessions—especially Lincoln's things: his double-edged razor, the lidded pot of Old Spice shaving soap with its residue of dried, flaking suds. The bone-handled shaving brush made of silver-tipped badger fur hanging on its own silver stand. Wooden shoe trees that kept his saddle shoes from ever developing a personality of their own. The glass ashtray on Lincoln's dresser commemorating the Rancho Esperanza Country Club Seniors' Tennis Tournament, with Chicky's father's name engraved on the sterling silver rim. It held coins, white golf tees, and a yellowed ivory pocketknife I must have opened a hundred times just to run my thumb across the blade. I was trying to figure out what it was to be a man, I suppose, and was looking for clues anywhere I could find them. It certainly wasn't in their bedroom, where the twin beds were covered with pink-and-white flowered spreads and heavy linen sheets that Rosa, the maid, pressed in the mangle that took up half the laundry room. The only place I found any real evidence of Lincoln's manhood was right back in the kitchen. Here the freezer was stocked with wild ducks he had shot—mallards, teals, sprigs, gadwalls, and "spoonies"—preserved in gallon milk cartons with masking tape labels, and filled to the brim with frozen water to prevent freezer burn.

The Crowells took the sporting life seriously, incorporating it emphatically into their home décor. Both sides of the wide hallway leading into the mahogany-paneled dining room were lined with English prints celebrating the hunt. The intelligent, alert, purebred eyes of those silently braying packs tracked me as I moved through the empty house, tingling with the thrill of trespassing. I read and reread the curious description under each engraving: *Pheasant shooting—La Chasse aux faisans.* "*Get Away Forrard.*" *Breaking Covey. Anxious Moments.* Antique hunting dog portrait plates were arranged on the wall above the dining room sideboard. In other rooms, all available wall space was taken up with richly framed paintings of hounds, spaniels, setters, and terriers. If all this canine imagery wasn't sufficient to convey the household's devotion to their four-legged friends, on every fireplace mantel and bookshelf sat pairs of Victorian Staffordshire spaniels—posing ceramic versions of Best in Show.

The mood of the place was enlivened by the Crowells' "collections"—proof they felt no need to impress. I'm speaking of Chicky's snow globes commemorating her various travels, domestic and abroad, and Lincoln's ducks—wind-up waddling duckies, rubber duckies, hand-carved wooden decoys, a duck pitcher with parted yellow beak spout, and all sorts of other duck-related kitsch that could have come right from the little tourist trap of my hometown.

Roaming through that vast house and looking at their things only made me more curious. I used to wish I were invisible so I could follow the Crowells through each and every room and see what actually took place in their cushioned lives. I wanted to know what they talked about when they sat on the terrace with a cocktail in the cool of the evening, watching the deer shyly pick their way out of the redwood grove to drink at the pond.

I wasn't the only one who was curious. Even people who *have* money are intrigued by people who have *more* money. This revelation took place at the local YMCA, where my mother thought

I should go to be around men who might serve as role models. On my first visit, I found myself in the Jacuzzi sandwiched between two bosomy old guys in ballooning bathing suits who were boasting to each other about how much money their sons made. I piped up and mentioned I lived at the old Stokes estate because I thought it conferred a special status on me. "I hear they have a full-time staff of six," one of them said. The other asked me if it was true that they dressed for dinner every night. I had no idea what "dressing for dinner" meant. Only years later did I realize he probably didn't either, and that it was the old guy's assumption of how Old Money lived that had prompted the question.

Some of what I knew about the Crowells' personal taste I had gotten from my mother, who confided some of Chicky's dictates. Although they were inconsequential matronly matters, inexperience led me to believe they were the Rules of the Rich: Never have yellow flowers in your garden. Always dry pillowcases in the sun. It's vulgar for women to wear jewelry during the day, except pearls. Serve brown toast for breakfast and white rolls for dinner. Ladies use nail buffing cream, not colored nail polish. Candles, bedding, and napkins should only be white or ecru. Never break bread with the help. Never.

Because my mother was well-spoken and white, Mrs. Crowell treated her with a lot more discretion than she used with the head gardener or his wife. Manuel and Rosa lived in the Santa Lucia Valley, a few miles from the little Danish outpost where my mother and I had lived, and every weekday morning they drove over the mountain in Manny's old Ford truck, arriving at the estate at seven-thirty. More than once Chicky told my mother she would no longer allow Mexican couples to live on the property because their Catholicism kept them from exercising birth control and *good-common-sense*. "They have too many babies and they turn the gardener's cottage into a little Tijuana. You've got to be firm with them, like children," she'd say, "or they'll *just-keep-multiplying*." In a town that had seen its share of eccentrics, Chicky was known for her impolitic declarations and, like everyone who dealt with her, Lincoln took the path of least resistance.

Lincoln Crowell, whose lineage was less lofty than his wife's, was more democratic because of it. His manner was gentle and he treated the help, including me, with affable courtesy. Like Chicky, Lincoln rarely used my name. When we were together he called me "M' Boy."

"How are you doing, M' Boy?"

"Say, what does M' Boy think of this?"

"How'd M' Boy like to take a walk around the property?"

For a long time I wished Lincoln Crowell had been my *real* father. I'm sure being adopted and then having my adoptive father die fueled this fantasy. I used to imagine what life would be like if Lincoln recognized me as his long-lost son and then married my mother. The problem was, I just couldn't figure out what to do with Chicky, and variations of her death occurred to me more often than I'd like to admit. Lincoln never overdid it as a father figure, but he *did* teach me how to tie a Windsor knot for my high school graduation, and once shared with me the addled adage about it being just as easy to marry a rich girl as a poor one.

Having taken his own advice, Lincoln didn't have to work for a living and, as far as I could tell, spent most of his time trying to get out from under Chicky's majestic thumb. He sailed. He played golf every weekend. During hunting season he rose at four in the morning and drove to his duck-hunting club with his English spaniel, Winston, and didn't return home until dark. He went on extended fly-fishing vacations and slept in rustic, mosquito-infested cabins he knew Chicky would hate. He took his horses trail riding, occasionally played polo, and, for a while, bred and sold Andalusian dressage horses—although Ramón, who lived over the stud barn, did all the training, tacking, worming, and mucking. Lincoln's involvement in breeding these horses pertained to buying, selling, and watching them procreate—a spectacle I enjoyed, too.

The actual act was handled by Ramón and Manny, who, like most Mexicans I knew, had a practical knowledge of things that moved—cars, trucks, lawnmowers, and horses. The first time I saw the stallion's confident strut as he approached the brood mare was unforgettable. His ostentatious ardor was, to say the least, an interesting indoctrination for a boy whose only experience with girls was playing doctor with Anika Petersen when we were five. I knew sex was nasty but hadn't a clue what it actually entailed. But now I had a front-row seat and I couldn't take my eyes off the mare's pulsating crevasse, dribbling and oozing with every *wink winkwink wink*—an equine Morse code that spelled *Come and get me. Come and get me.* Despite her unambiguous invitation, I felt sorry for the poor mare, her tail wrapped and held out of the way, and her upper lip caught in a "twitch"—a simple rope and stick device Ramón twisted as a distraction from the more annoying antics going on just behind her. There was also the matter of her little colt, who didn't want to leave his mother's side. I was put in charge of making sure he didn't inadvertently get kicked and injured, and I held onto his rope and tiny halter with all my might. The whole event was both embarrassing and enthralling, and it saved my mother from having to deal with that aspect of my education, which would have been even more embarrassing. I wonder now if Lincoln, watching his stud and the subjugated mare, ever felt gelded by comparison.

Unlike Chicky, everyone liked Lincoln because he expressed himself in upbeat declarative sentences.

"She's a *peach* of a gal."

"He's a *prince* of a man."

"What a *marvelous* car. "

"That's just *tops*!"

Although, when the occasion arose, he wasn't above using quaintly derogatory expressions, referring to a neighbor with longish hair and blue jeans as "a dirty rotten hippie," or a tax lawyer who left a lucrative practice to defend conscientious objectors as "a lefty New York Jew." But it was all said in such an amiable manner, an almost naive surprise at what he perceived as other peoples' unacceptable behavior, that you couldn't hold it against him. The only time I ever saw Lincoln deviate from this polite decorum was when the Crowells threw their annual Fourth of July party. His customary propriety diluted with margaritas, he would play the banjo and sing songs of horny toads or yeller dogs, which Chicky referred to as "Lincoln's off-color repertoire." My mother told me Lincoln had once "gotten fresh" with her when he was drunk but she firmly rebuffed him, and the next day either he didn't remember or chose not to. I didn't blame Lincoln for his indiscretion, and I was actually angry with my mother for not understanding how much Lincoln needed her. For all her emotional reserve, my mother had been openly affectionate with my father, and I couldn't imagine Chicky much inclined toward even hugging, much less the act necessary to have produced their only child.

Claire Crowell was ten when I first met her, a year older than I. The first thing everyone always commented on was her hair, whose soft curls caught the light and framed her face like an angel in an illuminated manuscript. Even at a young age, Claire had the patrician good looks of her mother, the easygoing charm of her father, and a precocious sophistication on sexual matters, about which I was clueless. Although I understood where *horses* came from and had deduced where *I* came from, it still didn't

occur to me people would "do it" other than to make babies—
maybe two or three times at most (unless you were Mexican, of
course). Not until Claire told me so.

Claire was also blessed with a physical grace. She was a ter-
rific swimmer who could do the butterfly with kick-turns off the
wall, a move I'd never seen in my inland community pool. Living on the Crowells' estate gave me access not only to their
swimming pool, but to the ocean as well. Those days in Rancho
Esperanza, people didn't worry about their children's safety, and
Claire and I could walk to the beach without Chicky's or anyone's
supervision. The Crowells maintained a "cabana," but it was more
elaborate than the name might suggest. It was a narrow two-story
structure, the downstairs consisting of a bedroom and tiny bathroom, the upstairs a kitchenette, a compact living room with fireplace, and a balcony overlooking the ocean where the grown-ups
could meet for cocktails and wave to their neighbors—the cabanas
being only a few yards apart.

A wooden raft was put out a quarter mile off the beach the
morning before Memorial Day and taken in the morning after
Labor Day, and it became a destination as exciting as any exotic
island. Winston, the English spaniel, swam with us, or more often
right on top of us, and as Claire and I lay on the bobbing raft he
swam in circles, biting at his own splashes. The sun would dry
the salt on our skins and I would watch with fascination as the
red welts from his nails would appear on Claire's long, tan legs
and arms, which were covered in golden peach fuzz.

Claire was always making up games—which one of us could
do the most sit-ups, who could dive higher, who could hold their
breath underwater the longest. She was very competitive, especially on the tennis court. Her serve was crisp and her strokes
effortless. She was also a very good rider, having learned how
to handle horses from the time she could walk. She rode an

Andalusian stallion who was over sixteen hands, and although he was very high-spirited, he was always a gentleman when she had him under saddle. Claire knew how to use her spurs and crop judiciously, but had such a soft feel of his mouth and such a balanced seat, she could ride him bareback and barefoot and still get him to do the Spanish walk.

Where Chicky was oppressively proper and Lincoln could be a little stiff and old-fashioned, Claire seemed to prefer the relaxed companionship of the help. Sometimes she would come into the kitchen and watch my mother prepare dinner. She even helped Rosa polish the silver as they chatted in Spanish. Rosa called her *Pajarita*—Little Bird.

Some of the happiest times were when Claire and I sat, knees touching, in the John Deere and rode around the property with Manny and his Chihuahua, Pirata, named for the patch of black over one eye. Occasionally Manny would sit in back with the dog and let me drive. Once, while I was behind the wheel, bouncing over the roots in the grove of redwoods on the edge of the property, Claire reached forward to brace herself, and I caught a peek of her budding breasts through the opening in her blouse. Her nipples were like little pink cupcakes, and all I wanted to do was reach out and touch them. For months after, or maybe it was years, whenever she was with me in the John Deere I drove straight for the redwoods and aimed for the biggest, gnarliest roots, but it never happened again. I wondered if she had one of those Morse code winkers down there, too, and if it would signal to me when she was ready.

Manny and Rosa had five children—three girls and two boys. During school vacations Manny would bring his older son, Alfonso, to work. Together they hoed and mowed and weeded and planted and watered and raked with a confident closeness that didn't require conversation. Alfonso had been born in Mexico and was a smart kid—good at fixing things—and you could already tell he was going to become a gardener like his father. The younger son, Ignacio, whom everyone called Nacho, was born in California, and even though he was only thirteen the first time we met, he had a self-assurance that seemed much more American. Nacho's green eyes weren't like anyone else's in his family, and unlike his parents he was quite tall. Lincoln Crowell used to tease Rosa about who the real father was. I thought Nacho had a manly way about him, especially with the Mexican girls in town, who seemed to flock to him. Even though he was "the gardener's boy," Nacho didn't treat Chicky with the kind of deference I was taught, but rather a cheeky insouciance my mother would have frowned on—"Hey Mrs. C, how you doin'?" Part of his bravura came from having a good singing voice and performing solo in his school's a cappella choir. The Crowells even attended his concert two Christmases in a row at the Catholic church, where the acoustics were particularly good. Chicky once told Manny that Nacho was going to go far because he was a "can-do boy." I remember feeling a pang of jealousy that he'd been able to elicit such an extravagant compliment, and I was sure it implied that I wasn't a "can-do boy."

One Fourth of July, when Claire was sixteen and I was fifteen, the Crowells gave their annual party down by the barn, that finally ignited my own desire for independence. My mother and I were invited, as were Ramón, Rosa and Manny, and all five of their children. It was the one holiday on which Chicky felt the American spirit of equality and dined with the help; although the help somehow knew not to mingle. It was a casual affair where everyone sat on hay bales or picnic tables covered with red-and-white-checked tablecloths under the oaks. At about seven-thirty, as the margaritas kicked in and Lincoln picked up his banjo, Claire asked if I wanted to walk to the beach and watch the fireworks from the cabana.

We stood side by side in the tiny kitchen making screwdrivers with frozen juice, skipping the four cans of water and spooning the orange slush straight into the Smirnoff. The weather had been clear and warm up at the house, but a fog bank lay on the coast, and when Claire and I took our drinks out to the balcony the sea and setting sun were filtered through a scrim of thick white air. We could hear the ice cubes in our neighbors' glasses as they stood on their own balconies, but they were figures cloaked in wet shrouds at a ghostly cocktail party. The idea of being invisible made me feel happy and safe.

Claire hadn't thought to bring a sweater and asked me to stand in front of her to block the cool breeze coming off the ocean. I offered to get her a covering from inside, but the sweatshirt was damp and the towel sandy, and she tossed them both on the railing. She put her arms around me and I could feel her shiver through my shirt. Her small breasts were against my back as she pressed into me for warmth, and I got an immediate erection. By the time the first red, white, and blue stars exploded in the sky and we heard the *ooh*s and *aah*s from the apparitions around us, Claire and I were kissing. I don't remember who suggested we go inside, but we ended up in the downstairs bedroom.

I was as excited as a stallion but a little slower to find the winker. It wasn't where I expected it, and as I fumbled around with inexperienced fingers and a complete misconception of female anatomy, it felt like my hand went off a cliff. It was much farther south than I anticipated, and I couldn't believe how soft it was, and downy. Then Claire touched me and I found myself erupting in volcanic delirium. It was as surprising to me as it was to her. Unfortunately, there was another surprise. The only good thing was that we heard Lincoln upstairs a few moments before he found us, and we'd been able to reassemble our clothes. But Lincoln was no dummy.

"What kind of a crum-bum are you?" he said to me, which in Lincoln parlance was akin to calling me a fucking punk. Although

I'd felt invisible, apparently I wasn't. One of the Crowells' cabana neighbors, seeing two young things making out on the balcony, had taken it upon themselves to phone Lincoln. I had no idea how to answer him. I couldn't even look him in the eyes and instead found myself fixated on the bridge of his nose and the telltale signs of salt crystals from the lip of his margarita glass, which attested to his finishing every last drop.

With customary efficiency, Chicky had Claire admitted and shipped off to boarding school by September. I didn't know anything about St. Paul's, except it was far away in Concord, New Hampshire. We couldn't even write each other because our mail went right into the Crowells' box at the Rancho Esperanza post office. I don't know whether Lincoln ever told my mother what her son had been up to, or whether my mother just chose not to mention it, which would have been her style. But in any event, no one ever spoke of it again.

I'd see Claire when she came home for vacations, but most often I'd see her from afar—taking a dressage lesson in the arena or playing tennis with her father or driving off to meet a friend for a movie. By the time she was a freshman at Bryn Mawr, Claire's life had changed considerably, and mine basically hadn't. She was dating rich boys who lived in homes with crushed oyster shell driveways and who had family connections that got them lucrative jobs after graduation. I attended the local community college, where I had sex with future aestheticians and dental hygienists—good solid citizens who'd get married, raise families, and resent the fact they could never afford to live in Rancho Esperanza.

When Claire came home from her junior year abroad, she requested the table be set with the silverware turned monogram side up in the European manner. That was bad enough, but she also brought with her a Princeton boy who had celebrated her birthday in a restaurant that served coquille St. Jacques in a real scallop shell. I thought this must be the height of sophistication, even though I hadn't a clue what coquille St. Jacques was. All I knew was that it sounded a lot more expensive than the tacos wrapped in greasy yellow paper on which I existed. Chicky and Lincoln were delighted with Claire's boyfriend and asked my mother to put together an outdoor lunch they would take to the redwood grove. The picnic paraphernalia was on the front steps as I drove my white Datsun home from class and stupidly managed to get into Chicky's line of sight. I was immediately enlisted to load the baskets into the car. "He's not your slave, Mother," Claire had declared in front of her Princeton boyfriend, and although she'd meant to defend me, it only emphasized my position there. How could I ever hope to compete for Claire when to Chicky and Lincoln I'd always be the cook's boy?

As soon as I graduated college, I escaped Rancho Esperanza and got as far away as I could, which due to financial constraints was all of five hours away. But when I pulled off the freeway, I saw Silicon Valley spread before me like some geeky Wild West and, for the first time in my life, I felt completely at home. With barely time to change clothes, I caught the personal computer wave and rode it right into the Internet. Even as I was experiencing the first dizzying rush of financial virility, I was making a vow to myself to never again set foot in Rancho Esperanza. I steadfastly refused to visit my mother, announcing that if she wanted to see me she had to do it on my own turf. She reacted in her usual stoic way and never insisted I come to the Stokes estate, and I never did. Christmas was spent with friends in Napa or skiing in Aspen or traveling to Europe. I didn't feel at all bad leaving my mother alone, which, of course, makes me feel very bad now. But my good fortune also freed my mother, who eventually left the Crowells' employ and moved to the coast of Oregon to be with her sister. After a few years of exchanging polite Christmas cards, my mother lost track of them, but the Crowells were never far from my thoughts.

I married and divorced twice and remain childless. Being the only son of a widowed mother, I never quite grasped the concept of family. When I was younger I couldn't sacrifice the time parenthood demands, and the inevitable constrictions it imposes looked claustrophobic. I felt I was still catching up on things I'd missed out on in my own youth. But now that I'm heading toward fifty, at times I'm sorry. When I'm skiing and see a father and his daughter sitting on the chairlift, her little legs dangling off the chair, I feel I've missed the whole point of life. Or when I take my lawyer and his young son out for oyster shooters and watch the way he clinks shot glasses with the boy, saying "Good *man*" before they throw them back, I'm touched beyond words. But then I remind myself that, unlike dogs when they get annoying, you can't just stick children outside with a pig's ear. I'm cordial with both my ex-wives, having been generous with their alimony, partly out of guilt. They both told me I didn't make a very good husband because I was too preoccupied with work. They were right. I was driven to prove myself to people who probably never gave me a moment's thought.

Rancho Esperanza has changed considerably since my boyhood. Dowdy Old Money and shiny New Money are aware of each other, but they're tucked into very different pockets. I don't know whom I dislike more. I certainly don't fit in with the doddering dinosaurs who condemn anyone driving a foreign car with a HEAL THE OCEAN bumper sticker as a liberal peacemonger. Nor do I like being around the newcomers—successful middle-aged men with soft bodies in soft sweaters, who get together every morning on the patio of Arpeggio to drink lattes and ogle the young girls.

Although these men aren't what *I'd* call appealing, the intoxica-
tion of their wealth and life's pleasures invariably turns the mood
sexual in an adolescent way, and I begin to notice that their
raunchiness increases with the number of men who join in. By
their station, acquired in the meridian of life, they've gained the
confidence they never had as young men. But they're as repel-
lent as they've always been, except now they're rich. When the
girls walk by in their low-riding jeans with delicate straps of thong
underwear peek-a-booing just above that entrancing posterior
crevice, you can tell these men truly believe—at least in that
moment—they have what it takes to make these young women
happy. But even with all their money, they seem completely de-
void of creativity and imagination and their performance is probably prescription only. Those taut flat bellies may arouse their
hypothalamus, but I would bet these men have about as much
sexual prowess as the women from the Gardening Club sitting at
the next table.

Nor do I find their wives inviting. It's my experience that women
begin to feel contempt for men just about the time men stop noticing them. These women know that no matter how fit they are—
and they do look a lot better than their husbands—they'll never be
able to compete with a young girl's body. They've lost their sex
appeal, and the only power they have now is returning their food
at restaurants. But these wives understand the bargain and have
struck a deal. In exchange for their lives of wealthy servitude,
they've replaced passion and romance with children, charities, and
creature comforts. I was hoping Claire's life had turned out to be
different. Or if it hadn't, I was hoping I could rescue her.

I'd lost touch with anyone who might know Claire's where-
abouts. But my Realtor Steve—Steve Farkey, who also covers the
local social scene for the *Rancho Gazette*—turns out to be a wealth
of information. Chicky and Lincoln sold their home about twenty

years ago. "They were getting to that age when both they and the house were beginning to fall apart." Unfortunately, they sold "just before the market really took off." It had been sold thrice more since and went through just as many remodels. Steve represented the last buyers, a Hollywood producer and his wife—Miss Philippines and a former CNN weekend substitute news anchor—who paid $50 million. On closing escrow they turned the stud barn into "a screening room that made the cover of *Architectural Digest*," and hired a stonemason to chink *La Casa al Loma* into the pillars of their front gate. They kept half the property for themselves and subdivided the rest. It's still the biggest estate in town, and even after all these years it's known to the old-timers as the Stokes estate, which certainly doesn't hurt the new owners' standing in the community, whether they know it or not.

Neither Chicky nor Lincoln gets out much anymore, Steve Farkey informs me. They are now living in a "*casita* with an ocean blink" at the Seven Oaks Golf Club, where they can have their meals brought to them by the clubhouse restaurant. Even though a gardening service is included in the association dues, Chicky issues directives as if the gardeners worked only for her. As for Claire, Steve recalls the Crowells had a daughter but he has no idea what happened to her. I know sooner or later I'll bump into the Crowells, but after a few weeks with no luck, I take a chance and dial a number I memorized thirty-five years ago.

"How *good* to hear from you," Chicky says in that emphatic way she has of talking. "How-is-your-*dear*-mother, *do* tell."

I fill her in on the last few decades as best I can, and then tell her that, by the way, I've bought a house in Rancho Esperanza.

"*Well*," she says, not showing any surprise at all, "you won't find it the same as when you left. New people have moved in and *things-have-changed*. Hollywood types bought our old house, you know, and they've *ruined* it. But tell me where you're living." I tell her I'm on Jacaranda Drive (in "the golden rectangle"). But once again, she registers neither surprise nor approval.

"You must remember the Shawls? They are *dear* friends who have that lovely Spanish colonial on Jacaranda" (she pronounces it "Hacaranda") "designed by Addison Mizner that is *just-a-gem.* Ollie Shawl's family came from Akron. They made all those rubber tires. His grandfather was a judge who came out here to retire and called Rancho Esperanza 'Ohio by the sea.' He and my grandfather started the Rancho Esperanza Country Club. I'm *sure* you remember them—Ollie and Danzy Shawl. They always came to our Fourth of July party. You remember our party? Well, we've gotten it down to just a few-good-friends and you *must* join us. Claire will be here and I know she'd love to see you, *as-would-Lincoln.*"

It doesn't seem like the right moment to ask if Claire is married, or maybe I just want to put off knowing for just a little longer. In any event, I accept her invitation.

"Manuel and Rosa don't like driving over the hill on holiday weekends but now that I know you're coming, I'm going to *insist-they-come.* Manuel and Rosa are *fine* people, you know. We're starting at *six* for cocktails and then we're going to the clubhouse at nine to watch the fireworks from the terrace. It's actually quite a good view, and you avoid all the parking problems at the beach. As you've noticed Rancho Esperanza has gotten *too crowded.* It's not the same place it used to be. So *do* get-here-*at-six.*"

When she mentions Manny and Rosa, I'm both amused and annoyed that her noblesse oblige has been reactivated for my benefit. As much as they're "fine people," I don't really want to be relegated to sitting on a hay bale with them reminiscing about Pirata and the old days.

I'm embarrassed to admit how much time I spend thinking about how I will present myself. I'm all too aware of the Crowells' standards, but they aren't my standards. I wear mostly jeans and

T-shirts, and my hair is a little on the long side, which in Lincoln's world would qualify me as a dirty rotten hippie. In the end, and only in deference to the Crowells' age, I decide to wear khakis and a button-down shirt. And I get my hair cut.

The Crowells' home is a one-story hacienda-style surrounded by white granite gravel that serves as a practical ground cover for the requisite cactus and succulent garden. The whole presentation has the planned and bland look of a gated community. Chicky answers the door and I feel an unexpected rush of warmth for her, and a definite impulse toward giving her a hug. But she puts a very firm hand out for me to shake, with not even a crook in her arm, keeping me about three feet away. Looking at her through the eyes of an adult, I see she must have been a real beauty in her day. She has grown a little thick around the middle, but her hair is now whitish blonde, almost translucent like baby's hair—once again justifying her name—and it's pulled back into a surprisingly girlish ponytail.

"How *good* to see you, kiddo," she says, looking at me with those intense blue eyes.

Standing in their new unimaginative house, recognizing the English furniture that no longer fits in with the surroundings, the dog paintings, and the stiff arrangement of sofas and chairs, I feel almost fond of Chicky for not wavering from her own archaic formality. It's both satisfying and strangely disappointing when I realize the Crowells don't have the taste or the money I once thought they had. I wonder if they know how rich I am.

"*Do* come and get a drink. We're all on the patio. And keep an eye out for those damn golf balls. I've had our picture-window-replaced-*twice*."

It's not a large backyard, but their borrowed landscape looks across the fairway up toward the mountains, and it's a very pleasant spot if you like golf. Chicky has decorated with little American flags stabbed into flowerpots set on the bamboo bar where Lincoln stands mixing margaritas. Gone are the hay bales and tables covered in red-and-white-checked tablecloths that I'd helped set up year after year. And where are all the people? The only familiar faces are Manny and Rosa and their son Alfonso, who all hover over some sizzling ribs on a built-in gas grill that seems too large for the yard. There are eight or ten people and children running around, but they're all strangers. They're all Mexican. A boom box sits on the grass playing Mexican music heavy on the brass, and I realize what's happening: the Crowells still think of me as the cook's boy, and have invited me with the help.

"Well well, M'Boy, well well," Lincoln says, only it comes out "Weww weww." He steps out from behind the bar and slowly shuffles toward me using a cane topped with a carved duck's head, and I realize he must have had a stroke. He's wearing lemon-yellow pants with no break, the hems riding two inches above his shoes, and his arms are thin now and speckled with dark bruises. "It's mawewous to see you." He gives me a hug with three firm pats on the back. He's so much smaller than I remember. I wanted to hug Chicky for her strength, as I now feel the urge to love Lincoln for his frailty. "Won't Cwaiwe be supwised," he says. "Whewe *is* Cwaiwe?"

Everyone starts calling for Claire.

"She must be in the kitchen," Chicky says, and I turn around as Claire steps barefoot through the French doors onto the patio.

"*There's* my *pajarita*," Rosa says.

She's still a lovely woman and I feel a huge relief, as if I've been holding my breath for decades. Her hair, that wonderfully curly halo of hair, is a darker blonde, and the skin around her eyes shows just the smallest signs of the outdoor athlete she still must be, but she has the same smile, the same girlish voice, the same lean body that looks perfect in the white shorts she wears.

"Hey you," she says, putting her slim arms around me, as best she can with a drink in one hand and a bowl of guacamole in the other. Two girls I would judge to be around twenty and sixteen follow in her footsteps, holding baskets of chips. One of them— the older one—has Claire's curly blonde hair and olive skin that almost glows in the sun. The younger one has long dark hair down to her waist. She, too, is lovely.

"This is Jennie and Catherine, and *this* is my friend Peter."

All kinds of emotions well up inside of me—a pang of regret that they're not our children, happiness at their beauty, a sharp sense of loss over losing my father, sorrow that my mother's life was so hard, anger at a childhood I wish I could redo. My eyes fill with tears and I put on my sunglasses so no one will notice.

"You remember Nacho?" Manny says, bringing over the can-do boy—a tall, good-looking man now, who I notice has a walkie-talkie clipped to the belt of his jeans. Jeans! "He's a fire captain now," Manny says with pride.

"Hey man," Nacho says, grabbing the muscle between my neck and shoulder and giving it two quick little compressions. "It's been a long time." He smiles with those white, straight teeth all the Mexican girls used to love. Then he puts the very hand that squeezed my neck around Claire's hip and right into the back pocket of her shorts.

Chicky turns to me as if we are alone and fires off one more of her characteristically spirited salvos. "I call this place Jurassic Park," she says with a wide gesture encompassing the neighboring houses across the fairway. "Just wait until we all go up to the clubhouse to watch the fireworks. All these people think I've turned their precious place into a little Tijuana. But see if I *give*-a-damn," she says, lofting her margarita glass with its sturdy stem and bright blue rim high above her head, like the Statue of Liberty with her mighty torch.

The Savior, Alfonso
Jerry Green

My father had an expression: "If you want to be happy, put your head up your *tuchis.*" This Solomonic pronouncement was always, at least in my memory, delivered during dinner in our Brooklyn apartment, where he sat at the head of the table with a small glass of slivovitz as my mother passed the stuffed cabbage. It was preceded by my sister or me bemoaning some random injustice we'd experienced. But instead of simple sympathy, we would get what my sister referred to as "Benny's Life Lessons." We can laugh about it now, but as a boy growing up, I resented his cynical Old World outlook. Why did he have to associate happiness with a ridiculous contortion, an image of some poor sinner in a Hieronymus Bosch hell? Why couldn't he give us, his children, the American blessing? *Go forth and be happy.* It wasn't until last night, forty years later, that I finally understood what Benny was saying.

Last night the hot, dry Santa Ana winds came, as they do every fall, just when fire danger is most extreme. Fifty-mile-an-hour gusts whipped up the oak and sycamore trees in my front yard, overturned a potted ficus, and tore the Italian market umbrella right out of its stand. I found myself lying wide awake, waiting for the sun to rise, thinking for some reason of my neighbor Sally Topping and wondering what Benny would've made of her.

Sally and Walter Topping live across the creek from my property. Walter started our local bank, the Rancho Esperanza Savings and Loan, and Sally, so she proclaims, has always enjoyed being a wife and mother. The most interesting thing I can say about Walter is that he gets all three of their cars washed and filled every Saturday right after golf. But Sally *does* interest me. Not that I'm attracted to her healthy, clean looks or long-legged stride. For me, her unrelenting happiness and her big, undiscriminating smile would destroy the mystery of sex. Sex with Sally, I suspect, is probably as matter-of-fact as doing a load of laundry or sorting the mail. The *mystery* of Sally is how she has escaped the ordinary miseries of life. Is she a fool who hides her head as Benny's homily suggests? Is it an indication of her virtue? Or does she somehow skirt misfortune and tragedy by pure dumb luck?

The Toppings have produced four fair-haired, blue-eyed girls—the twins are in high school with my son. When her children were curious, active toddlers, I don't think it ever crossed Sally's unburdened mind that they might wander out an open door and drown in the swimming pool, although she gave them every opportunity. As they began to mature, Sally couldn't imagine her hormone-deluged daughters would act out and blame her for some unhappiness, and in fact, they've all turned out to be as idiotically cheerful as she is. When each of them learned to drive, she never seemed to worry they'd get into an accident, and none of them ever did. This godly benevolence extends even to her golden Labrador retriever, who's allowed the run of the neighborhood. I'll see him darting about the road with a Taco Bell wrapper in his mouth or sniffing a beer can tossed out by construction workers, who show their contempt for the wealthy by leaving us their ample proletarian garbage. Doesn't she realize it's a miracle the dog has never been hit by one of their trucks speeding down our hill? Once my wife and I were hiking just above our house and saw Sally charging up the trail with such Bavarian purposefulness one almost expected a yodel. The dog, the four-pawed version of his mistress, was frolicking in the poison oak and foxtails, tongue lolling out of his mouth in a silly canine grin. We all greeted one another and I warned Sally of a rattlesnake sunning itself a little ways up the trail. But she dismissed any possibility of disaster with a wave of her hand. "Oh, Boomer's so oblivious, he just steps right over them." Fine, I thought. As long as the snake is equally oblivious. Me, I've taken my dog to a snake aversion clinic and watched the poor thing get zapped by electric shocks administered through a contraption strapped to its neck. When everyone else in town installs burglar alarms because of a rash of break-ins, Sally blithely leaves her doors and windows open, drapes a-flappin', inviting anyone with a gun and ski mask to come right in. But such things will never happen to Sally. Why? What would Benny say? This is what I pondered as dead branches and limbs from the sycamores flew onto our roof with disconcerting thuds. I kicked off the covers and wondered: Is Sally lying in her bed right now fearing a wildfire might sweep down from the mountains, leaving nothing but charred rubble and ash? Or does she somehow know the flames will leap right over her shake roof and land on mine?

Renee and I moved to Rancho Esperanza eighteen years ago. The property we bought was described in *Casa Elegante*'s glossy magazine as *a California craftsman style originally built in 1927, boasting a mountain view and seasonal creek on one of the most prestigious streets in Rancho Esperanza. This country house,* it went on to say, *will smother you and your guests in its thorough attention to artistic detail and Tuscan-like 1+ acres studded with mature California oaks.* Realtor's prose aside, the week we moved in, Renee and I felt sure we'd entered an enchanted land where time stopped at the freeway off-ramp. The town had only one traffic light back then, and two stop signs. It was Brigadoon by the Pacific, a green, leafy village suspended in very expensive aspic. We used to say that whenever a developer drove by, Rancho Esperanza would disappear into the milky fog rolling in off the ocean.

We were delighted by everything we saw, and everything we *heard.* The bells at the brown-shingle Episcopal church ring out three times a day: eight, noon, and six—breakfast, lunch, and cocktails. This quotidian comfort is interspersed with helpful reminders that life is precious and all too fleeting. I'm speaking of the ecstatic bells that proclaim a bride and groom have just been joined in holy matrimony. And the slow, sober tolling of the bells as the casket is carried past the calla lilies and out to the black-curtained hearse. What price can you put on the distant sound of a lonely train whistle when you're nestled under a feather comforter on a cold winter night? Or a great horned owl in the oak tree outside our library hoo-hooing at Charlie Rose? Even the coyotes howling in the field at the top of Star Pine Hill provide just the right rural touch. Although it can be a bit unnerving when the yelping accelerates into a high-pitched frenzy, and you know they're eating someone's cat. If you overlooked the food chain, Rancho Esperanza was too good to be true.

Then we met our neighbors. The majority of men seemed to be older, alcoholic Republicans with blue eyes and vascular noses, which made them look like they'd been snorting Bordeaux. At night, their old lumbering Lincolns and chrome-intensive Buicks would weave their way heavily along the dark, winding roads with their high beams permanently on. Who the hell cared that I was coming from the other direction and dimmed mine? In the local grocery, immaculately dressed, silver-haired women doddered to the checkout stand with nothing in their carts but Gordon's gin and Hostess Sno Balls. Renee felt she could never fit into such a lily-white community. I told her she was being too sensitive. But when she went to the hardware store to buy a mop, the cashier, taking in her dark eyes and olive skin, counted out her change in Spanish. On a perfect day, not a cloud in the sky, Renee would escape to her old life in smoggy L.A. and, while she was at it, pick up a couple dozen bagels. The move had been easier on me because I had a new business to run. But I wasn't immune to feeling displaced, although I could never admit it for fear she'd insist we move back. But back to where? After discovering the pleasures of country living, and there were many, I couldn't return to L.A. Besides, I'd closed the men's custom clothing store I'd owned in Beverly Hills, sold the building, and relocated my entire operation. There were many times back then when I wondered if I'd made a mistake. If we'd ever stop feeling like gefilte fish out of water.

Then the Clinton years came and the Old Guard in Rancho Esperanza spat his name in disgust, even as the New People moved in and real estate doubled, tripled, and then octupled in value. Today there are four traffic lights in town, arugula, radicchio, and tuna tartare on almost every menu, a supermarket lot filled with Mercedeses and BMWs, and a Democratic congresswoman elected by a landslide. Some of my best customers from the Beverly Hills days have even moved here. Unlike the parsimonious natives, or "cheapskaters" as Benny would've called them, they enjoy advertising their prosperity. This Christmas, the merchandise flew off the shelves so fast I was afraid my entire stock would be depleted before the end of the holiday season. Still, I regret the loss of the horse pastures, which have all been developed into *luxurious, private mini-estates offering the finest in country amenities.*

Sally Topping grew up here and takes it all in stride. Her father was the Methodist minister downtown and taught her to trust in the goodness of man and put her faith in God to watch over her. My father survived the Holocaust and taught me many things, most of it having to do with man being selfish and cruel. I'm not sure if Benny believed in God, but he believed in Fate, although he felt you could outwit it if you were shrewd enough. Neither school of thought particularly suits me, one requiring a genial passivity, the other necessitating eyes in the back of your head. So in times of greatest need, I've chosen to put my faith in Alfonso, my Mexican gardener.

From the day we met, I could see Alfonso was different from the others. The gardener we had before would dip his head and look up, addressing me as *Patron*, as if I were on horseback and he was toiling in my fields. This neocolonial relationship made me uncomfortable. I felt justified letting him go after he hacked away at the venerable oaks and overwatered their roots. Alfonso is respectful, but never subservient. He's proud without any of the macho swagger. And he's a big man, with strong limbs, rather like a sturdy oak himself. Our landscape architect calls him a "gentle giant," and that's how I've come to think of him, too.

"How old do you think Alfonso is?" I asked Renee one morning as through the kitchen window I watched him cutting back the plum tree with a surgeon's care and a sculptor's eye.

"I don't know," Renee said. "It's hard to tell."

"You think he's younger than I am? Or older?"

"I don't know," she said with diplomacy. "You know how sometimes you can't tell with Mexicans. Sometimes they *look* younger."

What Renee meant is that Alfonso still has a head of thick, buoyant black hair, although it's almost always flattened under a mesh cap decorated with fake bird droppings splattered on the bill. But my question had nothing to do with vanity. It had to do with my feelings toward Alfonso. I'm protective of him like a father toward a son, but sometimes when I'm with him there's also a resonance of my own childhood. That brute strength and immigrant determination reminded me of Benny.

When we moved to Avenue Z in Flatbush, one of the first things Benny did was plant vegetables. His garden was a three-foot strip of dirt wedged between the concrete driveway running behind the brick row houses and our own garage. Benny used to say, "You should never waste a chance." Benny's Life Lessons. Everyone else grew weeds but Benny had green beans, tomatoes, and two rows of corn, which he wouldn't pick until my mother made sure the water on the stove was at a *rolling* boil. Benny would have loved my garden, got a real thrill eating Fuji apples right off the tree. Picking tomatoes, Japanese eggplant, sugar snap peas, satsuma oranges, Meyer lemons, peaches, and red-fleshed plums. I'm only sorry he didn't live long enough to enjoy it.

On Monday and Friday, Alfonso's days, I go to work a little later so we can walk the garden. Not that I ever have to tell him what to do. He usually anticipates problems before I can even make the suggestions. When I have to go out of town on business during the rainy season, Alfonso will stop by the house to make sure the gutters aren't clogged. I even consult him on home repairs. When the garage flooded during El Niño, he and his men dug French drains. The flagstone patio he laid cost about a third of the stonemason's bid. He got rid of the rats that used to scurry across the roof, waking us up in the middle of the night. And when the dog cornered a rattlesnake near the woodpile, Alfonso killed it with a quick blow of his shovel, peeled off the skin, and hung the three-foot-long fillet in the sun for his lunch. So much for Taco Bell.

Over the years, Alfonso has saved me a great deal of money. But it's more than that. I'd much rather talk to Alfonso than any of my neighbors. With neighbors I wind up discussing real estate, remodels, or our children. And there are only so many times I want to debate the pros and cons of the Princeton Review versus the efficacy of private tutors. But with a garden there's always something new to consider and Alfonso has a certain amount of knowledge to impart. I felt there was a kinship, even a friendship, that had developed between us, so when Alfonso began calling me Jerry, it seemed perfectly natural. It would have seemed strange if, after all this time, he still called me Mr. Green. "Call me Jerry," I'd have said. But Alfonso anticipated that, too.

Alfonso takes care of my garden and I take care of Alfonso. I'm not only talking about the clothes and all the other things I'm glad to get rid of: the worn sofa bed, defunct computer, outmoded VCR, outgrown racing bike, slightly bent miniblinds, and low-flush toilets that have all been loaded into the back of his truck at one time or another. I also happily pay the tuition at Alfonso's son's school. When Alfonso's cousin had trouble with the INS, I put him in touch with an immigration lawyer and had the bill sent to me. Alfonso's Christmas bonus is more than a month's salary. I'm always saying to Renee, "He's so conscientious. He's the kind of person you don't mind helping. You *like* to help him. How else are these people going to get ahead?" I looked upon it as a mitzvah, a good deed. But I'm also counting on Alfonso to *be* there for me, too, come the conflagration.

Every fall, when the brush above our home turns crackling dry, and the wooden signs along the winding roads read FIRE DANGER TODAY: HIGH, I begin my vigil. Any smell of smoke, even from an innocent barbecue, sends me running outside to scan the sky. When the Santa Ana winds kick up at night, I pray there's no crazy arsonist, unattended campfire, flash of lightning, chainsaw spark, or car with an incendiary tailpipe parked over the wheat-colored grass. It doesn't matter where a wildfire is burning, Montana or Malibu, I watch the news over and over again, flipping channels to make sure I see every charred remain, every eerie, orange sky or lonely chimney left standing. Renee tells me I always expect something bad to happen, to stop being such a nervous Jew. But bad things *do* happen and loss *is* involuntary. I'm just trying to prepare myself, to get a plan of action so I'm not taken by surprise, like Sally Topping is going to be. I learned from my father, who lost everything, that you *deal* with it. He started over and over again and he never complained. When I was a kid, he used to say to me when I'd complain about something, "*Gornisht helfen!* Nothing will help. The Jews sat around Poland crying *Oy vay iz mir.* And look where it got them. *Action*, only *action* helps." Benny's Life Lessons. I know my house is only a possession, not an entire country, or a family you'll never see again. But I do what I can to make sure my moss-flecked shake roof doesn't end up as tinder, and my beautiful house mere kindling.

During fire season I call Renee several times a month from work and make her repeat to me the list of things we hope to save: family photos, pictures our son drew when he was small, a string of Mikimoto pearls I gave her when she turned forty, a small David Hockney, the Navajo rug we bought on our honeymoon, and all the other keepsakes we've collected that remind us of the time we collected all the keepsakes. But when the day finally comes, I know we might have just enough time to start the cars and grab the dog. Alfonso's the one who said he'd get there in time to pull the floating fire pump from the back of the garage. He's the one who'll attach the bag of fire retardant to the hose, yank the cord to start the earsplitting gas motor, and shlep the heavy contraption into the pool. He knows just how to soak down the roof and the oak trees because it has all been discussed. And rehearsed. Many, many times. And it also doesn't hurt that Alfonso's brother is the chief of our local fire department. I trusted

Alfonso would do everything possible to save my house. So it came as something of a surprise, a shock actually, when Alfonso made *the remark*.

We were walking around the garden and I was in a fog because I'd been up half the night waiting for my seventeen-year-old son, Ian, to come home. His curfew is eleven-thirty and when he wasn't home by midnight, Renee had already imagined him lying in a ditch covered in blood.

"I *told* you I was going to Zane's," he said, when I asked him where the hell he'd been. Maybe he had, maybe he hadn't. I honestly couldn't remember.

"What were you doing there until three o'clock in the morning?"

"I fell asleep watching a movie. Then when I woke up, I was *trying* to be considerate and not *call* you."

"It didn't occur to you I'd be worried?"

"I thought you'd be sleeping like any *normal* person."

"They were smoking pot," Renee said to me when I finally got back into bed. "Where were Zane's parents—little Miss Philippines and the husband with the pony tail? That's what I'd like to know. I don't like him going over there and I don't like that Zane. And I don't know why you put up with Ian's shit. He's always trying to get around you."

I knew she was right on all accounts. The next morning after she'd left for Pilates, and I'd gotten Ian up and told him his car privileges had been suspended, I drove him to school, then went *back* to the house and snooped through his room. Of course, I found the pipe, which he didn't even try to hide. Without thinking, I put my nose to the bowl and inhaled. At first it elicited an involuntary smile, and then a small, unexpected longing. I'm aching for my own youth, I thought. I'd smoked a few joints in my day, some hash, mushrooms, and even did a version of the

Hunter Thompson thing—driving cross-country in fifty-four hours
with my cousin Ritchie, nibbling acid the entire way. Now I drink
red wine for my heart and the most dangerous thing I ingest is
the fried calamari at Teocalli's. I sat on Ian's bed and lit up the
sticky remains. The taste was so familiar and good I wished I had
more than just the dregs. I managed to get two fairly good hits
when I realized it wasn't my lost youth I was mourning. It was
my father.

One of my first memories was the boat trip from Germany in
1949. My mother was seasick for what seemed like the entire
voyage. I only remember being with Benny. When the bells on
the boat would ring, for some reason I'd get scared and hold up
my hands and say to him, *Tateh, klingst, hantees.* Papa, ring,
hands. Even in the middle of the ocean, my father was still haunted
by the acrid smell of the ashes that had rained down day and night.
Now he was on his way to a new country, not knowing any English and having no idea how he was going to support his family.
His wife was belowdecks throwing up, and his two-and-a-half-
year-old cried every time the bells rang. And what did he do?
Complain? Yell? Cry? Shake his fist at the sky and curse his fate?
He took me by the hands, picked me up in his arms, and *com-
forted* me. I remember it distinctly. *Sha, boitshick, sha.* "Shush,
little one." He was probably thinking to himself something I'd
often heard him say in later years. *Besser dos kind zol vainen aider
der foter.* "Better the child should cry than the father." Benny's
Life Lessons. As I walked around the garden with Alfonso that
morning, half exhausted, half stoned, I was thinking not only of
my father but also of my son. What wisdom, what lessons can I
impart to him? If I talk to him he thinks I'm lecturing. Which is
why I had decided to let him spend a week with my sister and
her family. Let him knock around the streets of New York, I
thought. Let him see how other people live, appreciate that not

everyone is rich. But instead of just observing the lower classes, Ian came home imitating them—two gold-and-diamond-studded caps snapped on his front teeth.

My father, of all people, would have appreciated the absurdity. Although I hate to think what he would have done to me as a kid if I'd squandered money like that. But it's not the same with Ian. He knows we have money and he's never had to do without. In Benny's world you spent only on necessities. Everything else was for your children. I'm in awe, now, when I think how Benny had quit his job in the Robert Hall warehouse and moved us out to California because he thought there were better opportunities in Los Angeles. At the time I was in a teenage stupor, like my own son. I didn't realize what it must have taken for a man in his late fifties, with only a fourth-grade education and a letter from the Amalgamated Clothing Workers of America saying he was a member of good standing, to try and start his life over again. Of course, no one would hire someone his age, so he went into business for himself selling day-old bakery goods. My father worked day and night so his family could escape Flatbush, and my son wants to look like he just came from the Fulton Mall. So this is why I was more than a little distracted when Alfonso said what he said.

In trying to recollect it for Renee, I couldn't remember what had precipitated the remark. It seemed to come out of nowhere. "You have to be careful of the Jews."

"You have to be careful of the Jews. What is *that* supposed to mean?"

As soon as I told her, I regretted it. "I'm not saying he said it. I'm saying that's what it sounded like."

"I don't understand. You *think* he said it or he said it? Because if he really said it, I don't want him working for us."

"Renee, Renee, calm down. I could be wrong. He has a heavy accent. Sometimes it's hard to understand him. And lately I don't even hear you that well. I'm always saying, 'What?' Do you notice how often I say, 'What?' I'm losing hearing in my right ear."

"So what did you say when he said or didn't say it?"

"I didn't say anything. It happened too fast and then he pointed out some new gopher holes and went into the garage to get the traps, and by that time I wasn't going to follow him in there and start questioning him about Jews. And my own father used to say, 'Don't trust Jews.'"

"He meant *Hasidic* Jews."

At seventy-eight Benny was still working, selling over-bakes, recalls, and day-olds to the Mexicans and Hasidic Jews in downtown L.A. Everyone knew Benny's Day Old Bakery, right at the foot of Angels Flight. The Mexican walk-ins were only a part of his business. He made his real money on the standing orders from the Hasidim who owned the nursing homes. The Mexicans he liked, but he had no use for the black-clad Hasidim.

The Hasidim loved my father because he gave them the best prices and the best goods. They had a budget of thirty-four cents per meal, and what could you get for that? White bread and desiccated donuts. But Benny made sure the old people got *quality*. Little individual pies with maybe the crusts broken. So who cares? Bagels, rye bread, challah. My father made sure the old people *ate*. And then he'd spit when a Hasid walked out the door.

Like with everything, he had his reasons, even if they were twenty years old. Benny had been working in Long Island City in the Robert Hall warehouse, and on his way home he'd stopped by the Hasidic shul in Williamsburg to say Kaddish for his parents. But the Hasidim would have nothing to do with him. Who could be more Jewish than my father? His first language was Yiddish. His own parents had died in the camps. "These are the Jews who give Jews a bad name," he'd say to me when they'd come to buy his day-old bread.

I always try *not* to be the Jew who gives Jews a bad name. It's a gentile luxury to believe how *you* judge yourself is the only thing that really matters. So you can imagine how relieved I was when I remembered where Alfonso and I had been standing when the questionable slur was uttered. "Wait a second," I said to Renee, "now that I think about it, we were standing right in front of the garage and I realize what Alfonso said was, 'You've got to watch the *yews*.' We were right in front of the old *yew* trees." They're meant for colder, more northern climates and periodically I have to call a tree specialist who comes out and sprays them for fungus.

"So he's a yew hater," Renee said, happy as I was at the revelation.

Friday, first thing I did was to steer Alfonso back toward the tall, skinny trees. "So, how do you think the yews are doing?"

"They doing good."

"You don't think we have to watch them for that fungus?"

Alfonso took a supple branch and bent it in his hand for me to see.

"So far so good. They look healthy."

I knew then, I didn't want to know what he'd said. And I put it out of my mind for maybe three weeks or so. Until the wall fountain stopped working. Alfonso, without being asked, took the pump back to the store and about an hour later I heard him under the house installing the new one. I stepped into the courtyard for an update on the situation and he came out from the crawl space, cobwebs dangling from his mesh cap.

"I told them these pumps are no good," he said. "They get too hot. They burn out."

"So what'd they say?"

"They gave me a new one because I showed them the receipt, that it's still less than a year. But by only two weeks. They weren't that happy to give us a new one for free. We're lucky it burned out when it did. This other lady I work for, she called the manufacturer and yelled at them because she always has to replace the pump. She's a tough lady. She can really yell. She's a Realtor in town. You have to be careful of her."

"What do you mean?"

"Oh, if she's on your side she's okay. But if she doesn't like you . . ." He made a face. "She wouldn't let her own son stay at her house. She owns two houses and she was selling one. She made him go to the empty house and sleep on the floor. She's a mean *Jewish* lady."

I understand from experience how inconsiderate teenage children can be. And I wanted Alfonso to see other possibilities. That making your son sleep on the floor isn't necessarily a religious trait.

"Maybe she was afraid he'd ruin her house. Maybe he's too sloppy and she was having an open house the next day."

"He's not a teenager. He's already old. She's just a mean *Jewish* lady."

I never hide the fact I'm a Jew but neither do I advertise it to people who aren't Jewish. There's no mezuzah on the front door. I have no interest in such things. For Christmas, Alfonso receives his bonus in a Season's Greetings card on the front of which children are making nondenominational snow angels. My store is named Maxwell & Company, a tweedy revamping of my middle name. I've trained myself not to say *oy* when my back twinges, mostly because Renee makes fun of me when I do. And our last name isn't Jewish. My father took care of that when we first came to this country. So why would Alfonso suspect?

"I'll tell him I'm Jewish when the right time comes," I said to Renee. "I don't want to embarrass the man. And I don't want to lose him."

"*Lose* him? Who else would be as good to him as you are? You're paying for his son's *Catholic* school, for god's sake. I mean really, Jerry. You're like the poster boy for the good Jew. Just *tell* him."

An opportunity presented itself only a couple of days later. It had been raining all morning and I was just getting out of the shower when I heard the ladder hit the side of the house. I looked out the window and saw Alfonso below, taking the screens off the gutters. It was a Saturday, not even his day to be here.

"Jerry," he said, looking up at me, his hands cupping wet wads of leaves, "I have to ask you a big favor. I may need your help."

"What's the problem?" I saw on his face that something was wrong.

"This guy in town, you've heard of him, *Ornstein*? He's very rich. He owns a lot of properties. I bought my house from him five years ago and I couldn't get a bank loan and so he said to me, 'I'll give you a loan but I'm not doing anything to fix up the house. You buy it *as is*.'"

With a name like Ornstein, Alfonso must have known he was a Jew. Did Alfonso think this Jew was a Shylock? "What kind of interest is he charging you?"

"Eight and three quarters."

"What'd you pay for the house?"

"A hundred and seventy-five thousand, but since then I put on a new roof and I painted it and did a lot of work. Now I think it's worth maybe two hundred twenty-five thousand. I got a letter from him saying that my lease is up and now he wants the rest of his money."

"What do you mean, your *lease*?"

"I don't know. I thought I had a loan with him and I pay him every month early so I won't be late. They say he likes to take back houses he sells. He has a bad reputation. So maybe he's trying to take my house away. What do you think?"

What I thought was that Ornstein *does* have a reputation in town. He's a developer who has sued the county and is always at odds with the architectural board of review. But Ornstein also sponsors Anne Frank Week and promotes a conference on tolerance given in our local schools. Could Ornstein have such a moral disconnect he'd try to screw a gardener out of his home?

"Did he send you anything about a balloon payment? Have you received any default notices?"

Alfonso shrugged. "I received that letter in the mail but I don't know what it means. It just says my lease is up."

I told Alfonso to get all of his loan documents together and drop them off at the store. Nine-thirty that night, after Renee had already eaten dinner and called to say she was going to bed, I finally got a chance to sit down and write Ornstein a letter.

Alfonso was alarmed by a request for a full payoff of the loan, as it is contrary to the loan terms represented to him. He asked me to look at the loan papers and contact you on his behalf. The enclosed All-Inclusive Note Secured by Deed of Trust shows a 10-year term beginning August 2001, indicating the loan does not become due until 2011. We assume this incident is a misunderstanding on the part of your representatives.

The truth of the matter is it *could* have been a misunderstanding. Alfonso had received and promptly lost the critical letter Ornstein supposedly sent asking for full payment. Two days later, I got a call from Ornstein himself. "I never told anyone in my office to send him a letter. As far as I know, the loan is due in five years."

"I hope Ornstein isn't mad at me now," Alfonso said when I told him the response.

"Don't worry about it. And let me know if he sends any more letters."

"Thank you, Jerry."

"So did you tell him?" Renee asked me.

"It wasn't the right time."

Last month, at the beginning of the school year, I once again paid the tuition for Alfonso's son. He's a quiet, good-looking boy around eleven or twelve years old, but without any discernible personality. It's very hard to engage this kid in conversation, and believe me I've tried. I'm always met with a blank expression on his face, and he never looks me in the eye when I talk with him. Who knows, maybe he's just shy, but, as Benny used to say about people with awkward social skills, "I don't think he'll make it in retail." He rakes the sycamore leaves in slow motion. He's afraid of the dog and turns his back when she tries to play. Sometimes he kicks a ball in the dog's direction but never with any enthusiasm. "He's lazy," Alfonso tells me, laughing. "The girls work hard. But he doesn't like to work." Still, he brings the boy on school holidays and during the summers he's out there on the lawn watering the hot spots. I don't feel sorry for the kid having to drag a hose around. I also had my first job when I was eleven. Only I really *worked.* First delivering flyers door-to-door and then at twelve delivering groceries. I worked so I wouldn't be a burden to my parents. I worked so I could buy my own clothes. Especially the shirts at Jimmy's European Fashion on Kings Highway in Flatbush. My father couldn't understand why I'd prefer Jimmy's shirts to the shirts he could get me at Robert Hall.

"You're paying ten dollars for a *shirt*? *Bist meshugeh*? I could get you the same shirt with my discount for a dollar fifty! What are you wasting your money for?"

How could I explain to him the difference in tailoring? The difference in *feel*. How could I explain how much I hated that Robert Hall jingle?

> *School bells ring and children sing*
> *"It's back to Robert Hall again."*
> *Mothers know for all your clothes*
> *It's back to Robert Hall again.*

But it was the *other* cheery refrain that annoyed the hell out of me. *Low overhead! Low overhead!* Even at twelve I wanted style. Not low overhead.

"If you're going to spend money like water you better get a *real* job," Benny told me.

When I was in college, I worked for my father one summer. That was a real job. At five-thirty in the morning he'd be banging on my bedroom door for me to get up, and by six we were in the delivery truck making the rounds of all the bakeries. It wasn't so easy getting those boxes of bread into the truck, believe me. One-pound loaves, fifty of them, sliding this way and that. My father would push me out of the way, and lifting the box with hands that looked as big as tennis rackets, he'd say to me, "*Here, this* is how it's *done*."

When we'd come home around six, my mother would have dinner on the table and then around eight or nine, when the Jewish bakeries on Pico and Fairfax were closing, we'd make the rounds again. My father always knew how to get the best merchandise. Any fool could buy recalls. That took no brains. And who even *wanted* recalls? Recalls were iffy because you never knew when spoilage could set in. And mold was bad for business. But with the over-bakes, there was nothing wrong except there were too many of them. *That* was the merchandise you wanted to get before your competitor. When the plant manager asked five cents a piece for the over-bakes, Benny would offer him twenty bucks for the whole load, and then give him "ten dollars for your trouble."

Then one morning we came in to one of the bakeries and they'd changed plant managers. Maybe they thought he was giving away the shop, who knows? All I saw was that the one we knew wasn't there anymore, and now we had to deal with the Aryan from Bakersfield, this big, blond *dumkop* who scared the hell out of me. *A shtik fleish mit tzvei eigen.* A piece of meat with two eyes. The first day he said to Benny, "You Jews are always looking for a bargain."

"So? Who doesn't want a bargain? *You* don't look for a bargain *too*?"

"Yeah, but not like you *Jews*. I don't make a *career* out of it."

I just wanted to get the hell out of there, but my father very calmly conducted his business, his hands going deep in his pockets as he jingled the quarters. It was a gesture I'd seen how many times before? As soon as Benny's hands went into his pockets and he deliberately jingled the quarters, I knew he was assessing. He kept quiet until we were loading the goods into the back of the truck. And even then, the only thing he said was, "Wait, wait. He'll come around. They always do."

My father took his time and slowly, slowly, he won over the blond Aryan from Bakersfield. Slowly he corrupted him. I watched how my father operated. It was never overt. It was "ten dollars for your trouble. It's *understood,*" Benny would say. "It's understood." Benny's Life Lessons. By the end of the summer, the new plant manager was practically *throwing* the good stuff our way. That was the first time I ever really appreciated my father.

I'd taken my coffee outside into the garden and I was looking forward to reading the paper. Looking forward to a little peace. But Alfonso's son appeared by my side holding an order form and a three-ring binder. I knew the routine because we go through it at the start of every school year. He was selling wrapping paper as a fund-raiser. And I end up buying more than I can ever use as a way of supporting him. It's always the same generic paper with silver snowflakes or Happy Birthday balloons. It ends up crammed in the hall closet, falling at my feet every time I look for a jacket.

"You feel like buying some wrapping paper?" This was addressed to a Valencia orange tree.

I thought, Alfonso's son could use a summer with Benny. My *own* son could use a summer with Benny.

"How you liking school this year?"

"It's okay."

I opened the binder and flipped through the familiar selections. Birthdays. Holidays. All Occasions. I found exactly what I was looking for and read off the order numbers to Alfonso's son, who carefully copied them onto his form.

"You won't get it until the end of October," he said to a pot of rosemary, and I went inside to write him a check.

October is the month I dread most. The mountains have been baking in the heat for the entire summer and all it would take to ignite the tinder-dry sagebrush is a cigarette flicked out a window by a construction worker speeding down our hill. I keep my vigil, nose to the wind, and call Renee from work so she can go through the list of things we hope to save.

The hot, dry Santa Ana winds are right on schedule, blowing across the desert, over the mountains, and in through the bedroom windows. I stayed up most of last night. Waiting. Thinking of Sally Topping sleeping soundly in her bed. Even though we live just across the creek from each other, it might as well be an ocean. Sally's world is filled with cheerful children, a playful golden Lab, and an inviolable home. It wasn't until dawn, as the sky began to lighten and the winds finally died, that I figured out what Benny would've said about her, and what he was trying to tell my sister and me all those years ago with the head up the *tuchis* remark. He was giving us permission to be sad. He was saying it's better to feel pain and fear than to pretend it doesn't exist. Hands deep in his pockets, quarters jingling, he would've concluded Sally Topping wasn't a fool. Sally Topping has never been touched by evil. That's why she can't imagine the possibility of ashes raining down upon her.

This morning, through the breakfast room window, I watch Alfonso's men raking up the debris. The pool is full of leaves and I know I should get out there and skim it before they fall to the bottom. I hear rapping on the glass of our kitchen door and Alfonso stands on the flagstone patio holding a supermarket bag.

I open the door and he takes out three rolls of blue-and-white wrapping paper festooned with large yellow menorahs and dreidels. I thank him, and put the paper on the counter.

There's a moment of awkward silence, or maybe I just perceive it that way. Alfonso picks some dried leaves from the potted ficus. My hand goes into the pocket of my khakis and fingers the change. Then we get back to the familiar business of gardening.

"You want me to replace the lavenders, Jerry? They're getting woody. I can cut them all back but they're not going to grow back full because they're too old. They have five-gallons up at the nursery. It's much cheaper than the fifteen-gallons."

"You can put in the fifteen-gallons," I tell him.

"Are you sure? The five-gallons are much cheaper and they grow really fast this time of year, especially after the rains."

I tell him to put in the fifteen-gallons anyway. "And Alfonso," I say. "I've decided it's time you got a hundred dollars more a month."

"Thank you, Jerry," he says, looking pleased but not that surprised.

"So did you tell him?" Renee asks when I mention the raise.

"It's *understood*," I say, sounding like my father. "It's all understood."

New Blood
Sally Topping

Walter and I just celebrated our thirtieth wedding anniversary last month and we decided to have a little celebration at the Rancho Esperanza Country Club because we know six people who died this year and you just never know. Uncle Abner was well into his nineties and his Parkinson's had gotten quite bad in recent years, so his passing was actually a blessing, but the others weren't that old at all. One of them was only fifty-eight, just a few years older than Walter, and he owned a very successful insurance company right here in town. He'd been in good physical shape, went biking and running all the time, and had just spent two years (and I'm sure a lot of money) building this big, beautiful house he and his wife, Jane, had just moved into. One morning he said good-bye to Jane, went to work, and died of a heart attack right there in his office as he was putting together an umbrella policy for Danzy and Ollie Shawl. Danzy said he turned ashen and just went. That's why I think everyone should learn CPR, although apparently it wouldn't have helped in this particular situation because it was so massive. Also, Danzy and Ollie are in their early eighties. Danzy has emphysema, so she has no breath, and Ollie has had two knee replacements, so getting down on the floor was out of the question. Fortunately Jane's window washer, whom we've both used for years, remembered where Jane was going that day, and the police tracked her down at her bridge class. When Walter phoned to tell me the news, I could feel the hair on my arms just stand up in shock. Walter and I were so shaken by the whole thing, he finally got a colonoscopy (which he'd been putting off) and I bought three more place settings of our sterling pattern. For years I wanted to have sixteen place settings that match but I just kept saying to myself, Sally Topping, nobody really needs sixteen sterling silver place settings. At Thanksgiving and Christmas you can just mix it with the stainless and who will care? But after the terrible news, I thought, sterling is something I really enjoy and my girls will divide up the silver when we're gone, so it's not as if it's all going to end up in some stranger's breakfront. Walter's colon, it turns out, was as clean as a whistle so we gave this anniversary party to honor our friends and family and our good health and fortune.

For private parties at the club you can reserve the library off the main dining room. The library (used mostly by the wives who play bridge) overlooks the first hole and always reminds me of one of those quaint little parlors you'd find in an episode of *Masterpiece Theater*. The hand-screened wallpaper, showing a Chinese landscape with birds and pagodas, was probably very expensive when it was first put up. It's faded now as are the dark green curtains trimmed with little yellow-and-green ball fringe, but I think that's what gives it its charm. When we first joined the club in 1975 everyone seemed so old, although they were probably younger than Walter and I are today. Of course, now most of them are in their seventies and eighties, but the women are still going strong, like Danzy who's very active in the Gardening Club. Last week she gave me the most interesting tip: if you put a capful of gin in your tulip water, the stems won't droop as the flowers open. I tried it and I can't believe how well it works—much better than pennies. Unfortunately, the men haven't faired as well, and some of them, like Ollie, are so bent over you just wonder how they can still play golf. Walter says most of them *don't* actually, and the ones that *do* play only nine holes. But you have to admire them for getting out there and trying.

I don't play golf or participate in the club activities because I sit on two boards and am involved with a number of nonprofits in town. Although I love volunteer work and find it very gratifying, it does take up a lot of time and it has its own tedium. I mean, to me it *is* a job, which I'm always reminding Walter. Also, Walter and I eat at home at least three nights a week so I'm shopping and cooking, plus we have a subscription to the symphony and the Civic Light Opera. Not to mention the charity events we really have to attend because either I'm involved or we know so many other people who are. So I really enjoy my Saturday mornings in bed when the twins are still asleep and Walter gets up to play at the club. I treasure that solitude. Walter would like me to take up golf though so we could go on golfing vacations, but I'm not one of those people who think husbands and wives should do everything together. The clubs he hopefully bought me four years ago are still gathering dust in the garage, and the pink pom-poms covering the woods now look like dirty little baby hats. I feel very guilty about it. I tell him, "We can still have golfing vacations but I'll just go out and explore on my own." Like when we went to New Zealand with the Langdales. The inn where we stayed had lots of sheep, wild turkeys, and magnificent elk, and Merry and I got to take nice long walks while Walter and her husband played golf. For me, travel is all about seeing something different and meeting the people. If you're on a golf course all you're doing is walking around and searching for your ball.

We've been members of the Rancho Esperanza Country Club ever since Walter graduated from Stanford Business School, although because we were under forty we had a junior membership, which is a lot less expensive. To get into the Rancho Esperanza Club you usually need a certain social standing, and also to know five members who will write letters of recommendation. Walter thought it was important businesswise for us to become members, and although he was a newcomer to Rancho Esperanza, I suppose they must have seen his potential. Also, my father *was* the Methodist minister in town for a number of years. We never thought about anyone's social standing when we were growing up. Mother had to make do with the homes the church provided for us. Sometimes the church ladies on the Parsonage Committee would even tell her what color paint she had to use. If she wanted a yellow living room and the Parsonage Committee didn't approve of yellow, or didn't like the *hue* of yellow Mother had chosen, we didn't have a yellow living room. But Mother was quite a rebel in her own way, so she'd put up yellow curtains, which the church ladies couldn't object to because Mother made them herself out of the household budget they'd given her. Once, they painted my brother's room a shade they called beige but was actually pink. When Mother explained it was for a boy's room they still insisted *that* was the color they wanted. The church ladies were really quite tyrannical and acted like they had a moral aesthetic and Mother bristled every time we changed ministries and she'd have to deal with a new set of ecclesiastical decorators. But everybody in the congregation just loved Daddy because he was so accepting and open, and that's how I've tried to live my life. So that's why I think they ought to open up the

club to some new blood. But I don't feel it's up to me to say anything. It really should be Walter. As I mentioned, I don't go to
the club much, but Walter loves their prime rib and Yorkshire
pudding, and sometimes before the theater we'll go there for dinner. If you tell them you have an eight o'clock curtain, the maître
d', Arturo, always makes sure you're out on time.

My daughter Trish's May wedding is going to be in the library
but it can only accommodate 180, so it's going to be extremely
hard paring the guest list down. I just hope my relatives from out
of town don't all decide to make Rancho Esperanza their vacation. Then there's the groom's family, which I understand is pretty
extensive. It seems no matter how you try, when you give a wedding there are always people you have to leave out and feelings
get hurt. The Seven Oaks Golf Club can actually accommodate
many more and we've attended some lovely functions there, but
Walter prefers our club.

We just love the boy Trish is marrying. Webb works for
Deutsche Bank, something to do with lending money globally.
According to Walter, it's a very responsible position, which is
why Webb gets sent all over the world. After the wedding, Trish
and Webb will be living in San Francisco and I think it will be so
much fun visiting them. Trish is going to try to find a job in public relations like she's doing in L.A. I really couldn't be happier.

Except something happened last night that just put me into such
a state that I canceled my committee meeting this morning. I was
supposed to be chairing but I just called everyone and said I was
sick and wouldn't be able to make it. I feel so irresponsible
because now we'll all have to get our schedules reorganized—
not an easy feat with busy people. Walter is in Sacramento with
his mother, who has to sell her house because there are just too
many stairs, and he won't be calling this morning because they're
out looking at retirement homes. And the twins are on a school

overnight until Friday. So I decided to pretend it's Saturday and stay in bed a little longer, because I needed some quiet time to "commune with my innards," as Daddy used to say.

Yesterday morning all I was thinking about was Trish's wedding. Trish had made some appointments to look at wedding dresses in Beverly Hills and we arranged to meet in the shoe department of Neiman Marcus. Although she said I could sleep over at her and Webb's apartment so I wouldn't have to drive home the same night, I told them it wasn't necessary. I could tell Trish and Webb were just a little bit relieved because if I'm around it kind of puts a damper on things. When Walter and I were their age we already had two children and had to schedule a time for sex, which for most of our marriage was every Wednesday night and Saturday morning. We never even held hands in public because Walter is just not that kind of person. Trish and Webb are always showing affection and I think it's perfectly great. Now, in retrospect, maybe I should have stayed with them. I could have gotten up early this morning, gone right to my meeting, and this whole thing would never have happened. Instead I told her I didn't mind driving back, and not to worry about me. Walter does worry because he thinks I'm a terrible driver. That's just because I have so much on my mind I tend to get distracted. And sometimes, as I've explained to him, the object is below my line of vision like that metal pole outside my hairdressers. It's to prevent you from hitting the retaining wall but unless you know the pole is there, it can actually be a hazard. He's actually very good-natured about the car repairs and it has made for a lot of "Sally jokes." Like at our anniversary party when Walter got up and said, "I knew I was going to marry Sally when she backed my Jaguar XKE into a tree and then worried that she'd hurt the tree."

I don't ordinarily shop in Beverly Hills but Trish knew exactly where she wanted to look. After we found each other in the shoe department, we went up to the second floor, where we were helped by the most immaculately groomed Chinese woman. She was very petite and dressed in a navy blue St. John's knit with a cream silk blouse, and her black hair was done up in a chignon, which Asian women can wear so well. Her earrings were South Sea pearl and diamonds, which I don't think were costume jewelry because they looked absolutely real. No one dresses that way in Rancho Esperanza during the day unless she's going to a luncheon. To be quite honest, I felt like a big, overgrown country mouse. But Trish just loved all the attention and picked out four beautiful gowns from designers whose names I can never remember. We were ushered into a large white-carpeted dressing room with a plump sofa and a coffee table on which went a cappuccino for Trish and bubbly water for me. Of course, Trish was very careful with the coffee and didn't get it anywhere near the dresses. The Chinese woman, who was trying to make the sale, couldn't do enough for us and ran down to the shoe department, appearing with shoes that made Trish look about six feet tall (although I don't know why anyone would pay so much for a pair of shoes). There was one dress Trish liked that was kind of Grecian and the fitter was called in, a stout Slavic woman with straight pins on her cuff, who nipped in the waist and pinned up the hem, showing what it would look like when it was properly altered. "What kind of bra would she wear with this dress?" I wondered aloud, and the Chinese woman magically produced two pusher-uppers shaped like Cheshire cat grins. "These give beautiful décolleté," she said, and slipped them down the front of Trish's dress, positioned them just so. An impression of cleavage appeared, surprising even Trish, who takes after me in that department. "Beautiful, beautiful," the Slavic pincushion (Trish's description) kept saying to Trish's reflection in the three-way mirror, and the Chinese woman added her own retail flattery (Trish's description), "She look like movie star." I was a little unsure how we were going to tell them we still had appointments at other places and we didn't know if this was really *the* dress. I was starting to feel very responsible the more persistent they got, but Trish knew just how to handle the situation. She asked the saleswoman for her card and said she would call by the end of the day. Then we went to Barneys, which is a store I really don't understand. Even the way they display clothes is a bit odd. Most of the mannequins don't even have heads. Then we went to a bridal shop on Wilshire Boulevard where we found just the most darling dress that has tiny little peau de soie buttons up the entire back. I told Trish she'd better allow plenty of time to get into it. Then we had lunch at an Italian restaurant and went *back* to Neiman Marcus to try on the first dress, which the Chinese woman had put on hold. Trish wanted to make sure the one with all the buttons was really the one she wanted, and it was. The Chinese woman wasn't quite as gracious after we told her, but it was really a lovely mother-daughter day—although a bit exhausting. Trish is my first child to get married and I'm having so much fun planning this wedding. Pattie probably won't want a big formal affair—she's already told me she doesn't want to wear a veil—and the twins think big weddings are a waste, and they'd rather have the money for a down payment. They're both so practical for sixteen-year-olds, and I think it's very responsible of them. I'm sure Walter has had an influence.

After shopping and driving I wasn't in the mood to cook, so I got off before my usual exit because I thought I'd stop at Arpeggio and pick up a Cornish game hen stuffed with apricots and raisins, which honestly I couldn't do better myself. I parked right in front of the restaurant, and was getting out of the car when someone called my name. I turned around and saw Nacho da Silva headed for the same place. Nacho and I met singing in an interfaith choir. I consider my voice to be a nice soprano, but Nacho's tenor is exceptional—he's actually our main male soloist. Last year he sang the most beautiful *Ave Maria* I think I've ever heard. The choir even puts out a very professional CD for Christmas that sells quite well—partly because of Nacho, who has a little bit of a following in town. He's also quite good-looking, tall and slim with wonderfully white teeth, a very easy laugh, and posture that's just the tiniest bit stooped, as if he's bending down to really listen to what you have to say, which I've always found endearing. I think he could have become a professional singer but he's chosen to be a fireman, an extremely admirable vocation. When I was still jogging—before we got Boomer and I started hiking, because Labs need so much exercise—I used to see Nacho running around the track at City College in blue shorts and a T-shirt, carrying his walkie-talkie, and I'd think to myself, "Now there's an attractive man." His wife is just darling and his two girls are adorable.

When Nacho asked how I was, I told him I'd been shopping all day with Trish, and Walter was in Sacramento with his mother, so I was picking up takeout for myself. He told me his wife and two girls were visiting his parents in Santa Lucia, so he was getting a Cornish hen, too. We stood on the sidewalk chatting for a few minutes and then he asked if I'd like to go out for a drink before we picked up our hens. There was no particular rush for me to get home and I was all dressed up from shopping in Beverly Hills, so I thought a glass of chardonnay would really be nice after a long day.

Arpeggio doesn't have a bar per se, so we decided to go across the street to Teocalli's, which I've always found very cozy, although Walter doesn't like it because he thinks it's too dark and he can't read the menu without his glasses. And on weekends it does tend to get very noisy with a younger crowd. As we were waiting for traffic, Nacho looked very carefully in both directions, as did I, and then we naturally each put a hand on the other one's back, as if to guide each other safely across the road. It's the kind of thing I used to do with my children when they were small, and I'm sure he does it with his, but anyone watching would have thought we were walking arm in arm. I was actually touched he would be that protective because Walter usually walks a bit in front of me and he whistles. Walter has always whistled and I have no idea why. I've known him since the tenth grade, but I can't remember when it started. Even at his father's funeral, he whistled as we were walking to the grave site. I'm sure it's something that calms his nerves, and you'd think after all these years I'd be used to it. But sometimes it can actually be quite annoying.

Teocalli's is known for all the different tequilas they serve, so Nacho decided we should sit at the bar and have a margarita, which they make from scratch. I don't usually have mixed drinks, and I don't know one tequila from the other, so Nacho ordered a margarita he thought I'd like with Damiana in it. He explained it was a liqueur that comes from a plant indigenous to Mexico, and that his mother swears by its medicinal properties and has a small glass every night before going to bed. I have to say, it was the best margarita I've ever had. Thank you, Mrs. da Silva. After one drink we decided to have another, then we moved to a booth so we could order dinner, although after the margaritas and chips I wasn't that hungry. But I didn't want to leave because I was finding Nacho the easiest person to talk to. He kind of reminded me of Daddy in that way.

"Walter and I are actually quite different," I told Nacho, because we had naturally gotten into a conversation about our families. "Trish and Webb, my future son-in-law, are living together, which Walter and I of course didn't do before we got married, being a Methodist minister's daughter. I've known Walter since I was in the tenth grade, although I didn't start dating him until I was a junior in college. Even though Walter's only a year older, at first I used to accept his opinions as if he knew more than I did. When we were still engaged, our first disagreement was over Richard Nixon. I said, 'I'm voting for Hubert Humphrey and I'm a Democrat and you'd just better get used to it.' I don't think Walter ever heard me talk that way before. I think he was in shock, quite frankly." Then I explained to Nacho that we'd solved the problem by not talking politics. And all our friends know not to bring it up either. "I don't expect everyone has to be like me," I said. "Walter is much more reserved than I am and he's very thoughtful before he speaks. Everything is said in very measured tones. I just blurt everything out. But as my father would quote from the Psalmists, '*We're fearfully and wonderfully made.*' We're all different and unique, but that doesn't mean one is better than the other."

Then Nacho said something I didn't expect. "Ever since I first saw you I've wanted to know you better, but it seems like we never really had the opportunity to just sit and talk."

"Well," I said. "Here we are."

"Yes," he said. "Here we are."

We just looked at each other for what seemed like a minute, not saying anything, and I noticed he had the most beautiful green eyes, which were so attractive with his skin color and dark hair.

"What are you thinking?" I finally asked him, because it seemed like he wanted to say something.

"Have you ever smoked grass?" Nacho asked me. "Have you ever done anything the least bit subversive?"

"I smoked a cigarette once," I told him. "I was studying for an exam in college, but I couldn't see my book because of all the smoke and I said, 'This isn't for me.' I mean, I didn't have sex in college either, but that didn't stop me from having plenty of dates. I didn't even drink in college because the Methodists didn't drink back then, although they've loosened up in recent years. I have done some daring things, though," I said, "but mostly with nonprofits."

"I think you're probably the purest, most innocent grown woman I've ever met and you'd be so much fun to corrupt," he said.

"What do you mean?" I said.

"What do you think I mean?".

"I don't know," I said.

"I *mean* I want to do things to you. Things you've never done before."

"Like what?"

"Like I want you to go into the ladies' room right now and take off your panties."

"What?" I said.

"Take off your panties and bring them to me. I want you to come back to the table with nothing on underneath your skirt."

"You want me to bring you my *panties*?" I asked him.

"Please don't make me say it a third time," he said.

As far as sex goes, I had pretty much "closed up the shop," as Mother once said in a candid moment when explaining why she and Daddy slept in separate rooms. Although Walter and I haven't gone geographically that far, after thirty years with the same person and four children, there are honestly other things more interesting to do with my free time. Besides which, ever since Walter had surgery for a torn meniscus, he can't kneel, so I always have to be the one on top, and if my allergies are acting up, my nose won't quit dripping. I don't find it very sexy having a Kleenex hanging out my nose, and although we've never discussed it, I'm sure Walter feels the same.

On the bathroom wall of Teocalli's, right next to the sink, is a 1940s black-and-white photograph from the *Rancho Gazette*. It shows four beautiful young women dressed in lovely party gowns, standing in front of the old music pavilion at Casa de las Flores. They were each holding a silver tray with cocktails and the article explained that because servants were off fighting the war, the girls had been recruited to help serve drinks. I'm sure I must have seen that photograph at least a thousand times and never really gave it a moment's thought. But last night it struck me that the photographer had captured them at just the peak of their beauty, and I wondered what had become of them. Had they all gotten married? Had children? Had they realized their dreams? Were they still loved? Did any of them ever have a dalliance with a man they hardly knew? I don't exactly know why, but I kissed them, putting my lips to the glass of the picture frame. Maybe because I wanted to bless them for looking so happy and alive. Then I stepped out of my underpants. I looked in the mirror and said to myself, "Sally Topping, what in heaven's name are you doing?" But my face stared back and all it did was smile.

Instead of facing the wall as he had been, Nacho, to my surprise, had changed seats and was now looking out at the restaurant. The waitresses were so young and pretty, all about Pattie's age, probably students at the university, and even though it was October and turning cool, I couldn't help noticing every young woman sitting at the bar was wearing something summery. So many long, thin arms and bare midriffs, you'd think they'd just come in from the pool. There I was in a cashmere sweater set feeling very old, and it made me wonder—at what point in a woman's life does she stop dressing for men and start dressing for weather?

"Now sit beside me and give me your panties," Nacho said, and I slid in next to him. He put my panties briefly to his face and then slipped them into his jacket pocket and I thought, "Oh my goodness, where is this going?" But after only a few moments, I didn't care. I could have bumped into anyone I knew, and what would I have said? How could I possibly have explained what I was doing sitting next to a younger man, drinking margaritas with a look on my face that said, "Don't stop." When the waitress came by to ask if we wanted another margarita Nacho said, "Just the check."

He opened the passenger door for me and I got into his car, which was extremely clean. No children's things in the backseat or old Starbuck's coffee cups littering the front console, and I was very grateful for that. The seats were black leather and smelled clean, like they'd just been buffed with polish and, for some reason, I was grateful for that, too. He leaned over and kissed me, softly at first and then more passionately until his hands were underneath my shirt and in my bra and I suddenly knew how my own daughter must feel with Webb. I began to breathe rather heavily, which surprised me because I honestly didn't know I was still capable. Then Nacho started the car. "Where are we going?" I asked.

"You'll see," he said.

I found myself in a public parking lot downtown. Nacho drove around and around all the way up to the roof. I'd parked there thousands of times before, whenever I went to the Civic Light Opera, or a board meeting, or a movie—it's a very popular lot, and I'd always paused to admire the view from the top level before rushing off to do something.

"I've always loved the view from up here," I told him.

"Let's go look at it," he replied, and when we got out of the car, he took my hand and led me between some cars to a half wall where we could see the lights twinkling from the houses on the hill in the distance. I couldn't help thinking of all the people having dinner and watching the news and helping the children with their homework, and I was so glad, for once, I wasn't one of them. The parking lot lights gave a pretty pink glow and the moon, just a sliver of a thing, was rising.

"Look at Venus, how bright she is," he said, as he slowly lifted my skirt. He stood behind me, very, very close. "You asked me in the restaurant what I was thinking," he said in a soft voice. "*This* is what I was thinking." Then he stooped forward, as if he was listening to what I had to say, but I said nothing. I could feel his warm breath on my neck as he whispered things to me: a story about a woman who meets this stranger in a restaurant and what they do together, and things I can't really remember because it was filled with the most imaginative, wonderful details and words Walter could never bring himself to utter out loud. I was aware of shoppers coming back to their cars and motors starting and a car coming up the ramp, and I knew it would be searching the aisles for a place to park. It briefly crossed my mind that maybe there were security cameras, and I prayed anyone driving past would think we were just an ordinary couple who had stopped to admire the view. Except I could feel myself being lifted up onto my toes with every thrust, and I was grasping Nacho's hands to keep from screaming with joy.

The answering machine was blinking when I got home and I knew one of the calls had to be Walter telling me about his mother's retirement homes. Instead of playing the messages, I ran a bath, turned off all the lights in the room, and lit a scented candle. I stepped into the tub as the hanging chimes on the patio began to ring, and then the rustle of the sycamore trees filled the night with sound. Instantly the air lost its chill and the Santa Ana winds gusted through the open windows. I could still feel Nacho and kept getting a floating sensation, like shooting up in an elevator and leaving your stomach ten floors below. I lay in the bath and as the warm breeze caressed my body, I closed my eyes.

I saw myself in the blue chiffon dress I'd bought for the thirtieth wedding anniversary party we'd given at the Rancho Esperanza

Country Club. I was standing by an open window in the library. There were beautiful, long afternoon shadows on the fairway of the first hole. I turned around and saw everyone we had invited. They were all having cocktails before dinner. I stepped out to the terrace to admire the view and there was Nacho in a white summer jacket, which looked so good against his skin and green eyes. He was standing by the railing as if he'd been waiting for me.

"I want you to take off your panties," he said.

"We have to be careful," I told him. "My husband is just inside and there are so many people here I know."

"I don't want you to wear panties when you're with me. I have to be able to touch you anytime I want," Nacho said.

When I exited the powder room I had nothing on underneath my chiffon dress. He took my hand.

"Where are we going?" I asked nervously.

"You'll see," he said, leading me up the stairs to the small private banquet room on the second floor.

I could feel his warm breath on my neck and as we kiss his hand slowly, slowly lifted my dress. Nacho gently leaned me back onto the table and I became the banquet he consumed with his hands and his mouth. I knew dinner would be starting and I had to return quickly or my presence would be missed. I found this strangely exciting. But I also felt so irresponsible not being there to help seat everyone. Then I thought to myself, "Sally Topping, you're being ridiculous. This is just a fantasy and you can do whatever you want."

So I stayed in that banquet room with Nacho and let him do exactly what I think I've been waiting for my entire life. But when the bathwater finally cooled, it was time to blow out the candle. "Goodnight, Nacho," I said. Then I put on my robe, went downstairs to the kitchen, made myself a cup of hot water and lemon, and called Walter.

The King and Queen of Zirconia

Leigh McHugh

It's hard to believe now, but there was a time when my husband and I considered Howard and Nancy Berry close friends. We vacationed together, we spent evenings and holidays at each other's homes, we were even included in their son's wedding, where we were conspicuously seated at the table of honor. We were treated like family, part of the Berry clan. All in spite of the fact that we never really liked the Berrys, and the Berrys didn't entirely like us.

Although we lived not a mile from each other in Los Angeles, we'd met Howard and Nancy serendipitously on a Baltic cruise, the first night out of Copenhagen. It was only by chance we were even on a cruise—I'd won the trip renewing my pledge to a public radio station.

"Why would I want to be held captive, surrounded by a bunch of fat, old people talking about their heart stents and grandchildren?" Mac said when I proposed he come with me.

"Because when else will we ever get the chance to see the *winding, cobbled streets of Tallinn, and the charming little island of Visby, and St. Petersburg in the glorious midnight sun?*" I said, reading from the glossy cruise line brochure. "Besides, we don't even have to talk to anybody. At meals we can sit at our own table."

"Did you see there are two formal nights?" he said, pointing to the dress code requirements. "I don't want to have to wear a tuxedo."

"Why don't you try looking at it as a free vacation to a lot of places we haven't been before?"

"Because a cruise isn't my idea of a vacation. It's my idea of a floating prison."

We were standing in line at the pier in Copenhagen waiting to board when the ship's photographer motioned us to an easel holding a white life preserver with the cruise line's name stenciled in bright blue letters. "Smile!" she said to Mac. "This is your vacation!"

"God, this is depressing," he said to me, refusing to stop for the requisite photo. He was unhappy and short-tempered but there was nothing I could do to help him. I was all too familiar with these moods and, quite frankly, I was a little nervous about us spending that much time together. I knew we could very easily find ourselves in an argument that spanned the Baltic Sea, and I'd end up chronically apologizing for having insisted he come. So it was with some trepidation that I accompanied him to the Crow's Nest that evening to have a drink and watch the "sail away."

We found a little table for two by the windows and I noticed a couple seated next to us, their plates filled with a selection of complimentary hot appetizers. Even from a sidelong glance, I could tell they were not like most of the other passengers—Mac had been right—who were elderly and obese. The Berrys were our age and didn't strike me as the kind of couple who would dress up for the Fabulous Fifties Party, or stand in line to take photographs of the Midnight Dessert Extravaganza Buffet.

"Try the Thai spring roll," Nancy said, turning to me out of the blue. "It's actually quite good. Don't you think it's good, Howard?" she queried her husband. "But make sure it's *hot*," she said back to me, "and get the chili sauce with it."

Within minutes the Berrys informed us they had one son, Ward, who was a junior at Brown, let us know the cost of his tuition— "But he loves it so *much*," Nancy said, "we should be paying them *more*"—and told us what they did for a living. Nancy was an events organizer, and being a professional party giver seemed to suit her hysterical good cheer. At first impression she was a very attractive woman, but she had the kind of features that photographed better than they actually looked. A couple of things— nose and teeth to be exact—weren't even her own. What made her stand out was her willowy height—almost six feet in heels— and a sense of style all the more apparent on a ship Mac christened HMS *AARP*. Not only that night, but whenever we saw her, she was sleekly dressed and adorned with bold, brightly colored jewelry—turquoise and coral, amethyst, aquamarine, and peridot. The message she transmitted was as easy to read from across the room as it was sitting next to her. "I am rich," she beamed. But the tendency to jabber on without waiting for a response, and the odd habit of repeating herself—"Why did I eat all those nuts? I'm a bad girl. I'm a bad girl. Ooh. Ooh"—made her resemble an exotic parrot carrying on an animated conversation with its mirror.

Howard Berry was a business manager with clientele in the entertainment industry, and he managed to mention most of them within the first half hour of our acquaintance. Although he was at least three inches shorter than his wife, he was lucky to have a slim, athletic build, and a head of thick salt-and-pepper hair, which

Mac envied in private. At the end of one Absolut martini—"We always have a martini for the sail away"—and after he established we had voted for Clinton, Howard proposed we ask the maître d' to arrange a table for four. Although Mac and I had agreed we'd eat alone, I quickly accepted Howard's invitation, thinking the Berrys would be a distraction, if nothing else.

They couldn't have been more ingratiating that first evening, or more anxious to establish their credentials. Nancy, in particular, wanted to impress upon us that she and Howard were cultural cognoscenti. She *swooned* over Murray Perahia's Bach keyboard concertos, championed small dance companies—"The Smuin Ballet is first-class, first-class"—and let us know they had season tickets to the L.A. Opera and the L.A. Philharmonic and belonged to a nonfiction book club, but apparently still read the latest novels, as well as Trollope, *three* of whose hefty tomes she intended to reread on the cruise—"To *me* Trollope is *better* than Dickens." The Berrys were also au courant on Hollywood movies, as well as foreign films, and had just gone to the Indian Film Festival in Santa Monica, Howard pronouncing the Apu trilogy "phe*nom*enal filmmaking." It was hard to figure when the Berrys had time to sleep. As you'd expect, they made the yearly pilgrimage to New York, where they devoured all the plays and museums they could cram into their hectic schedule. One was tempted to think they took more pleasure in the regurgitation than in the actual feast.

I suspected their fervid cordiality had to do entirely with Mac, certainly not me. I was a mere fine arts instructor at Santa Monica College, teaching perspective and vanishing points to sleepy-eyed freshmen, while Mac, a chemistry professor at UCLA, had been instrumental in discovering a process by which plastic conducts electricity. Although the Berrys weren't interested in the science of it all, once Mac explained the practical applications of conductive polymers—flat screen TVs, mobile phone displays, computer screens, and the like, and mentioned he'd formed his own company, we became extremely appealing. Unfortunately, we didn't quite feel the same way about the Berrys. But after Mac finally got over being angry with me for accepting Howard's invitation, the Berrys did exactly what I'd hoped. Their drive for prestige and their need to distinguish themselves and be recognized as rich were so much fun to discuss and analyze, I don't know what we would have done without them.

"Oooh, looook," Howard had intoned one evening while perusing the wine list. "They have a Montevina Sangiovese.*"*

"We *loved* the Sangiovese in Toscana," Nancy told the wine steward, a young man from Budapest who hardly looked old enough to drink. Then turning to us, "We ordered Sangiovese every day. We never got tired of the Sangiovese in Arezzo."

Then there was the restaurant file Nancy had brought with her: articles compulsively clipped from *The New York Times Magazine*'s *The Sophisticated Traveler* and *Travel and Leisure*, organized by country, and assembled into a folder by her secretary. The Berrys took great pride in "discovering" those restaurants every time we arrived in a new port. "You didn't try the saffron *pannkaka*? Uh, we found the best place for it. It was fabulous. One of the *best* tastes I've ever had. Didn't you think so, Howard?"

The Berrys, hopelessly bourgeois, spent a great amount of energy defining themselves as haut monde, and to challenge them would have been pointless, as Mac reminded me: "Most people don't want to acknowledge the depressing tenet of relationships, which is if you want to get along in life and have any friends or family at all, you have to sublimate your desire for screaming out the truth. The smartest thing you can do is pretend."

I knew Mac was right, of course. Pretending was hardly a new concept for us. We went along with the pretense, for example, that Mac's older brother was the amiable paterfamilias of his extensive brood, a great guy, and a master of the bon mot. Because to point out how he batted away any serious attempt at conversation with strained one-liners, and how he hid behind his family and a pack of underachieving friends, would inevitably lead to the accusation that he was an angry man threatened by anyone economically and intellectually superior. We pretended his wife was a serious writer, although in twenty-five years the only project she'd ever completed, *A Unicorn Named Henry*, was an unpublished children's book. We pretended my college roommate was a wise family therapist when in reality she was a needy woman whose most obvious patient was right in her own bed— her depressed, passive-aggressive third husband, whom she ignored. We pretended this friend didn't marry for money, we pretended that friend didn't have fucked-up children, this friend wasn't gay, that friend wasn't an alcoholic, and on and on.

"Why do you think I find it so hard to have *real* friends?" Mac would say. "Why do you think I prefer being alone?"

But Nancy and Howard Berry, by comparison with most other people we knew, were cheerful and easy and, at first, it wasn't hard to pretend, right along with them, that they were who they pretended to be. Until the end of the cruise, when there was a small incident that exposed the Berrys and made it a little more difficult. We had all hired a taxi to take us into the center of St. Petersburg, and on the way I'd told them how Mac and I had sat on our veranda the night before watching that *glorious midnight sun*. I'd mentioned the veranda in an offhanded manner, certainly not to compare staterooms. After all, we hadn't even paid for ours.

"It's too bad our veranda isn't next door to yours," Howard had said in response. "We could have done that scene from *Private Lives*."

"We saw *Private Lives* with Juliet Stevenson at the National in London and I couldn't believe how *good* she was," Nancy added. "Howard and I were so surprised. You think of Juliet Stevenson as Hedda *Gabler*, but who would think she could do *comedy*?"

No more was said about our respective staterooms, and after spending the day at the Hermitage we returned to the ship in the early evening. Mac went to the gym, the Berrys stopped in the Java Bar for a complimentary cappuccino, and I detoured to the Photo Gallery to peruse the "Meet the Captain Night" photos for which we'd been obliged to pose. The Berrys had their backs toward me and never knew I saw them returning to their room, which was a little too close to the ladies' room and definitely *not* on the desirable side of the hall. Not only didn't the Berrys have a veranda, they didn't even have a window. Maybe, I thought generously, the veranda reference from *Private Lives* had been less a deception than their way of telling us, as with the saffron *pannkaka*, that they were in the know.

We arrived back in Copenhagen and exchanged telephone numbers but never really expected—nor did we particularly long—to see them again. We were ready for a vacation from the Berrys. But two days after we'd gotten home, before I'd even fully unpacked, Nancy called.

"I had an extra set of photos developed for your album. There's a *fabulous* one of you and Mac standing in that park in Visby, and wait till you see the ones Howard took of the nude beach in Warnemünde. What a hoot! I still can't believe Howard had the nerve. I'm on a *major* diet by the way, although I only gained five pounds, which was a shock after the baked Alaska and those Grand Marnier crepes. Tonight I'm just going to pick up a couple Reddi Chicks from the Country Mart and throw together a salad.

I just feel like something very *plain*. So why don't you come for dinner and we can look at the photos."

The Berrys, it turns out, were going to be our friends whether we liked it or not. Although Howard never grew on us, over the years we became rather fond of Nancy, and appreciative of the thought she gave our friendship. She always remembered birthdays, sent us books she thought we'd like, articles on subjects we'd discussed, and reviews of events we'd attended. This engagement in life through diligent busyness and Nancy's dependable conviviality livened up any gathering and garnered the Berrys a smorgasbord of friends. They had a friend in the leather business, a friend in the diamond business, one who got them Frette sheets wholesale, another with an "in" at Tumi luggage, and friends who remodeled an old farmhouse in Burgundy with an apparently charming guest room where the Berrys vacationed. They even had friends in New York with whom they usually stayed, who knew people who could get Howard an invitation to play golf at the notoriously exclusive Maidstone Club in East Hampton.

The Berrys lived well and looked richer than they actually were by being persevering shoppers, thrifty travelers, and connoisseurs of faux; the knockoff red Hermès Birkin bag Nancy carried, the two-carat cubic zirconia earrings, the ersatz Judith Leiber minaudière she'd gotten in Hong Kong. Howard's thick cashmere cable-knit button-down sweaters came from Costco, his ultrathin, preowned Patek Philippe watch was obtained through a connection at the L.A. Jewelry Mart, and his Armani suit was bought 60 percent off at the Barneys year-end sale. Surprisingly, they weren't the least bit coy about their purchases, probably because they knew we didn't care. If I ever complimented them on a new acquisition, they would happily tell me where they got it, how much it cost, and for what it had been appraised. Making me feel just a little bit stupid if we'd paid anything more, which Mac and I always had.

Whether about culture, politics, or travel, the Berrys' conversation was ultimately about money. Even Nancy's plastic surgeon, she informed me, was one of the most expensive doctors in Beverly Hills. (But, of course, she planned his wedding and was given a hefty discount.) At first I didn't understand why she'd asked me to take care of her after the facelift—Howard having fled to Palm Springs to play golf. Nancy certainly had a number of friends whose company she enjoyed more. Even as I whipped up banana, mango, and yogurt shakes, and pureed soups she managed to sip through a straw, it was clear the Berrys regarded Mac and me as their second-tier friends. I think they assumed anyone with money wouldn't be shy about exercising its power and they assumed Mac would want to parlay his financial success into social success. Because we didn't play along, we didn't excite them. Mac wore a cheap diving watch, he refused to lease a plane, he wasn't interested in joining a country club, and he disliked living in big houses. Nancy never understood, in all the years I knew her, why I had only a gold wedding band and not a walnut-sized diamond. Which, of course, is why she'd let me see her swathed and swollen black-eyed face. I wasn't someone whose judgment she had to fear.

But while Nancy could accept us as wealthy eccentrics, Howard began to treat us with a certain amount of disdain. As our friendship matured, not only did he stop trying to impress us, he punished us for not being impressed. At a dinner party in our home, he once brought *Conde Nast Traveler* to the table and, despite Nancy's remonstration, continued to read it right through dessert. Another time he got up from the table and took a nap on our couch.

Five years ago, we rented a four-bedroom "chalet" in Deer Valley with the Berrys, their son, Ward, and his new wife. It was owned by a movie producer Howard knew, and jammed to the old barn-wood beams with Navajo rugs, western saddles, and even an eight-foot-tall grizzly bear rearing on its hind legs. Mac thought it looked like the prop room of *Jeremiah Johnson*. It wasn't that we enjoyed spending time with Nancy and Howard, but they had made it easy—they got the house, they made the restaurant reservations, and they rented the car with their discount coupon. We found out later, quite by accident, that Howard had charged us more for our share of the rental than they'd paid. I'm sure Nancy hadn't a clue we financed their private ski lessons, as well as her son and daughter-in-law's, but I still held it against her for being married to someone who would do that.

At Mac's insistence, I didn't challenge Howard's creative accounting. "You're not going to change Howard," Mac said, being much too reasonable, "so what's the point of confronting him? You're only going to make yourself look foolish." But I was furious and wanted to finally let him know what I thought. "You want some kind of justice but you're not going to get it with Howard," Mac said. "It's not even worth thinking about. In the big L.A. pond, poor Howard's a small, ordinary fish who'll never be any richer or more influential than he is, and he knows it. He's koi polloi."

As always, I let Mac have the last word. Without explanation, I decided not to see the Pollois, as they came to be known, anymore. I thought it was going to be difficult extricating ourselves, but Howard and Nancy never even noticed. The Berrys, having done well in the stock market, sold their house in Santa Monica for three times what they'd paid for it—so they told everyone— and moved into permanent vacation mode. In true Berry fashion, they retired to Rancho Esperanza, where they found a house in probate and bought it for a fraction of its worth. At first, Nancy made a genuine attempt to keep in touch, but I made myself unavailable and our friendship quietly faded away.

A year and a half ago, my life took an unexpected turn. I said good-bye to Mac after twenty-six years of marriage. "I'm sorry I wasn't the husband you wanted me to be," Mac had said. It was one of the only times I can remember him apologizing. Although our marriage was far from perfect, Mac was the one person with whom I never had to pretend. I knew I would miss that terribly. Staying on in our house, with all the memories, was just too painful. So, in spite of the Berrys, I moved to Rancho Esperanza to begin again.

Although I made no effort to reconnect with Nancy and Howard, it turns out I didn't have to. My first Sunday in town, having breakfast at Smitty's, I found myself sitting next to an older couple who looked like they'd spent their entire lives drinking gimlets at the Rancho Esperanza Country Club. The woman was dressed in a cool blue sweater set and pearls, her silvery blonde hair worn in a ponytail. Her husband's watery eyes looked out from a face that was a compilation of pink, scaly skin and large, suspicious brown spots assembled on his pate and arms as well. As he shuffled off to the bathroom with his duck-head cane, I'd noticed the cuffs of his canary-yellow pants were two inches above his well-polished loafers, a look seemingly popular with a certain social set in town. Searching the restaurant for a sign of life or a Democrat, I spotted Nancy and Howard perched at the counter by the front door, each with a bowl of oatmeal and a section of the *New York Times*. Sometimes when you bump into people in a foreign country, you're often happier to see them than you would be at home, and discovering the Berrys here, in this new landscape, I felt a momentary surge of affection even toward Howard.

"I said I wanted *non*fat milk," Howard said to the Mexican busboy, thrusting a small metal pitcher back at him. I was waiting for the espresso machine to quiet down before saying hello, but seeing me at the far end of the counter, Howard, looking like a cashmere lumberjack in his Brioni buffalo plaid shirt, got up and ambled over.

"Oooh," Howard said as he stood over my shoulder and glanced down at my plate, "you got the Mexican awmlet." This was my greeting after all those years, said in that little boy way Howard adopted when he wants you to find him cute and loveable.

"I *heard* you'd moved here," Nancy said, her voice going up a couple octaves in excitement, as if she were delivering the most exciting news in decades. Then she, too, got up and in a moment they were both hovering over my breakfast. "Who *told* me? Arlene Fusco. Do you know Arlene? She's a weekend person here. We bumped into her at Arpeggio and she told me you'd moved here."

"I don't know Arlene Fusco," I said.

"So who told me? Who would've told me you'd moved here? How *are* you?" she said with sudden concern. I knew from her tone she was referring to the fact that I was now alone.

"Fine," I said, "great," because no one really wants to hear the lament of a middle-aged woman. Least of all Howard and Nancy.

"Aren't you *loving* it here?" she asked. "We were supposed to go on a cruise to Greece and Turkey in May. But I said to Howard, 'Why are we going back to Greece and *Turkey* again? Why don't we just stay *here* for our vacation?'"

"Oooh, stay heaw por bacation," Howard said, affecting a pout.

"If you're free tonight, come for dinner. Do you know the Kornblatts? Elliot and Cheryl? She's originally from Wilmington, Delaware, and had one of those childhoods where everyone went to cotillion and called their mothers 'Mummy.' You should hear her talk about it—she had me laughing out loud describing all her friends in their little white gloves. And he's this Jew from Columbus, Ohio, who made a fortune as some muckamuck at Lehman Brothers. They bought that Tuscan house at the top of Star Pine Hill. Actually, it's one of the nicest *new* houses I've seen, don't you think so, Howard? Fernando Laguna was their designer and he did a *fabulous* job making it look old. He had someone come in and faux the entire exterior with cracks in the plaster and darker shades under the eaves. He even put rusty nails and eucalyptus leaves on the terrace and just let it sit for a couple months until everything got weathered. It looks like it's been there forever. He did a fabulous job."

"You should see their apartment in New York," Howard said, suddenly quite grown up. "It's phe*nom*enal."

"We decided to all meet at Art Basel Miami and then we flew to New York on their plane to see their collection of modern art. Their apartment is e*norm*ous, fifteen rooms just off Park Avenue. But I have to tell you," Nancy said, discreetly lowering her voice, "I didn't love everything. I liked the Basquiats, but the Schnabels and Jeff Koons were just o*kay*. I mean, I appreciate them for what they *are*, but would I want to live with them *personally*? The one who supposedly has a *fabulous* art collection is Bobby Bingham. He comes from old New York money and is *quite* a character. He lives in the Casa," she said, as if I was familiar with the property, "and apparently he has an *amazing* collection of old French drawings. I'm *dying* to see them. He's coming tonight, too. We don't know him that well; he's an older man. How old do you think he is, Howard? Late seventies? Although he looks great. We met him at Seven Oaks where we play golf. Bobby always shows up at the club functions with a different woman. You should see all these women in their seventies—dressed beautifully by the way—drooling over him. He's actually *very* funny—don't you think so, Howard? He's definitely the hit of Seven Oaks with the women. He's got all the older women at the club *drooling* after him. It's a hoot!"

For all the hoopla over relatively little, Nancy's enthusiasm was appreciated. It reminded me of old and happier times. Moving to a new town and not having a dog, a school-age child, or a husband, my social life consisted mainly of conversations with people I was paying: the gardener, my contractor, the Roto-Rooter man, and various salespeople. I felt the Berrys were welcoming me back into the fold. Before they finally returned to their oatmeal, they'd shared the name of a masseuse, a reasonably priced landscape designer, and the best place in town to buy New York steaks. The only thing they couldn't provide was a cleaning woman. "Good cleaning women are hard to find," Nancy said. "It took me two years to find Fidelia, but she doesn't have any extra days or I'd take them myself."

The Berrys had written explicit directions on a Smitty's placemat, but I lost my way on the dark winding roads and was the last guest to arrive. Their house was charming, although I might have been surprised they'd chosen to live on such a modest scale, had they not told me its history. According to Howard, the house had once been part of a magnificent forty-acre estate named Casa de las Flores, built in 1907 by a St. Louis millionaire to lure his new bride to California. The property, Nancy went on to explain, had remained in the family until after World War II, when all its outbuildings and acreage had become a burden to the children. Consequently, the heirs began selling off parcels of Casa de las Flores bit by bit. The main residence, modeled after an eighteen-century Italian villa, was where Bobby Bingham lived, and was reportedly still quite beautiful, although its once legendary gardens were reduced to a mere five acres. Among the newer houses, with their media rooms and kitchen islands, some of the original estate buildings remained: the stables, the massive stone carriage house, the pool house, and the Berrys' house—known as the Music Pavilion—where the wealthy of Rancho Esperanza once came to be entertained in style. Being part of Casa de las Flores, being a part of history, the house had a cachet all its own. Mario

Lanza once sang for Charles Lindbergh right in the Berrys' very own living room. So said the Berrys.

Over the years, as I came to find out, the Music Pavilion had been tinkered with and expanded by its various owners—a kitchen and master bedroom added, and a garage with guest quarters built above—but the original Pavilion, with its high-beamed ceilings and wide-plank walnut floors, was still very much intact. Although Nancy and Howard didn't actually play any musical instruments themselves, they still referred to their living room, somewhat tongue-in-cheek, as the Music Pavilion. To emphasize its lineage, lest anyone forget, they kept an antique fruitwood music stand in the powder room, on which they hung crisp white Frette guest towels embroidered in cream thread with their initials *nBh*.

I entered the Music Pavilion that night as the Berrys, the Kornblatts, and Bobby Bingham were seated before an immense stone fireplace drinking mojitos, in honor of the Kornblatts' upcoming trip to Cuba.

"In New York we're out almost every night, except on weekends, when the bridge and tunnel people come into the city," Elliot Kornblatt was saying. "Then we invite a few people in and have our chef make dinner." In his mid-sixties, Elliot was dressed in khakis and a pink cable-knit sweater draped around his shoulders. When he turned his head toward the fire, you could see ancient pockmarks pitting his cheeks and the back of his neck, which mattered little now that he was old and rich. He spoke in a quiet, measured way, affecting some kind of cultured accent, although how he picked it up in Columbus, Ohio, I couldn't say.

Nancy introduced me to the assembled, explaining we were old friends and I had just moved to Rancho Esperanza.

"You're going to love it here but if you're anything like us, you won't want to live in Rancho Esperanza all year," Elliot said, addressing his comment more to Bobby Bingham than to me. "It's too provincial. It's a great place to have a house as long as you travel."

"We love travel," Nancy said. "Sometimes I think we travel *too* much."

Howard, in his buffalo plaid cashmere shirt, was smacking a nonperforming log, trying to excite some lazy embers into action. I'd remembered from our ski vacation that Howard took a manly pride in his fire-starting abilities, and spent a great deal of time with one foot on the hearth, poker in his hand. In Mac's opinion, Howard relied too much on newspaper, not enough on kindling, and didn't stack the logs to encourage airflow.

"*Great fire, Howard,*" Cheryl Kornblatt said in a no-nonsense way that immediately put you on notice she had definite opinions. About fires, and probably everything else.

"Tank goo."

"Elliot loves having a fire," Cheryl said. "He's like Richard Nixon. The air-conditioning on and the fire going."

"Cheryl thinks I'm extravagant, but I'm not quite *that* bad," he said.

"Well, you're not exactly Al Gore, either," she said, patting his hand with four or five quick taps, like a nurse reassuring her senile charge.

"As long as it's not those dreadful gas logs," Bobby Bingham said, repelled by the very thought. He was the picture of a prosperous, well-fed country squire: tan skin, round pink cheeks, blue eyes, and straight teeth that looked brand-new. But instead of sturdy corduroy and muddy Wellingtons, he wore black jeans and cowboy boots—a *Yee-ha!* look at odds with his manicured nails and gold signet pinkie ring. "If only the people with taste had money and the people with money had taste," he said with a weary sigh.

"The two faults I can find with *this* house," Elliot said, referring to his own home on Star Pine Hill, "are that they didn't think to put a fireplace in the kitchen and we don't have the wall space we need. We collect contemporary art," Elliot said, turning to Bobby Bingham and me, "and our house *here* doesn't lend itself to displaying it as it should be displayed. In New York we had someone from the Museum of Modern Art work with our interior designer to do our lighting. As Fernando Laguna is always telling us, 'Lighting art is an art unto itself.'"

"Howard and I are *dying* to see the Gerhard Richter retrospective at MoMA. Did you read the review in the *New York Times* today?" Then Nancy turned to Howard, who was balling up that very paper for his fire (Mac, you were right), which was now more ash than flame. "Howard, we have to go to New York before the Gerhard Richter show leaves."

"We're either going to have to start collecting Indian miniatures or we're going to have to move to a different house," Elliot said, not interested in discussing any art he didn't own.

"Bobby has an exquisite collection of French drawings that I'm *dying* to see," Nancy said. "Bobby lives in Casa de las Flores, with that *huge* wisteria vine on the front gate."

"Oh, I *love* your entrance," Cheryl said.

"Isn't that wisteria just *divine*?" Bobby said.

"It's *fab*ulous," Nancy said.

Nancy's conversational pomade dispensed, she turned her focus right back to the Kornblatts. "But you'd never actually think of *selling* your house, would you?" she said in mock disapproval.

"If something came on the market that had a view and the wall space and the fireplaces, I'd consider selling it. Tell them what you said about the firewood, hon. This is actually a very cute story."

"As you can imagine, we spend a *fortune* on firewood in Manhattan," Cheryl announced. "So I said to Elliot—only *kidding* of course—'If only we could take all the wood from the oak trees we just had trimmed *here* and FedEx it to New York, it would probably *still* be cheaper than what we spend.'"

"So we decided," Elliot turned to all of us, "to fly the wood back on our plane."

Howard sprung to life. "You're *kidding*? You're going to *fly* it back on your *plane*?"

Having gotten the response from Howard he was looking for, Elliot Kornblatt sat back on the couch and said no more.

"Before you came," Cheryl said, including me in this fascinating conversation for the first time, "I was just saying that we have about twenty oaks on our property and just the cost of trimming the trees *alone* could support a terrorist country."

"It's crazy," Howard said. "For what they charge you'd think they were doing cardiac surgery. Next time use *our* guy. He works for one of the tree trimming companies but he and his brother work for themselves on weekends and he's *half* the price. A couple a nice Mexican guys."

"Cardiac surgery would've been *cheaper*," Elliot said.

"Take a look at our oaks on the way out. They did a great job."

"Get his name," Elliot said to Cheryl.

"Before you leave I'll give you his number," Nancy said.

"Did Cheryl tell you what we paid to have our oaks trimmed?" Elliot Kornblatt asked Howard with a furtive glance toward Bobby. "When I opened the bill I said, 'This could support an *entire* Middle East terrorist country.'"

Elliot and Cheryl were the kind of people who had to work in their status within the first ten minutes, and did it with about as much subtlety as a cast-iron frying pan to the side of your head. But the Berrys, far from being put off by this, behaved like adolescents with their first crush. They basked in the glow of the Kornblatts' wealth as an affirmation of their own success. As if somehow the reflection—gilt by association—made them shine, too. The Berrys had always liked being around serious money, but since I'd last seen them, they'd become like salespeople in expensive stores who take on the mannerisms and attitudes of the people they wait on. The Kornblatts were the arrivistes lording it over the new arrivistes, and the Berrys were only too happy to oblige.

Bobby Bingham, being a single, sociable man and living in a grand house, was obviously used to holding court in Rancho Esperanza. It was no wonder he was popular with the older women at Seven Oaks. He was attentive, amusing, and—very important—ambulatory, although his delivery was a little on the bitchy side, which the ladies probably referred to as "his wicked sense of humor."

"Well. You *know* the story of your *wonderful* Music Pavilion?" he asked the Berrys, crossing one tooled black leather cowboy boot over the other.

"Mario Lanza sang for Charles Lindbergh," Nancy reminded us.

"Oh, yes, they had music here. It was *quite* the place to come for that, surely. But Mrs. Lillian Stevens, who gave those famous little soirées, was also known as something of a nymphomaniac." He leaned back in his chair, confident of the revelation's inherent melodrama.

"You're *kidding*?" Nancy said, rising deliciously to the bait.

"We *love* a good nymphomaniac story," Cheryl said drolly.

"Apparently," he said, with a teasing pause, "Lillian had a thing for the young, handsome workmen on her estate, shame on her. She had two daughters, you know. The *oldest* girl, Mercedes, was very ordinary-looking—looked just like her father, who owned a string of department stores in St. Louis. She died in an avalanche, skiing in Val d'Isère. But the *younger* one, Hadley, was *quite* ravishing and had more than a passing resemblance to a *certain Italian stonemason* who worked on your Music Pavilion. *This* is where Mrs. Stevens came to enjoy her erotic little trysts," he said, gesturing around the room. "Away from the prying eyes of the servants."

"Good for *her*," Cheryl stated.

"Hadley and I became dear, dear friends," Bobby continued, settling in for a longer tale, as the memories of Hadley Stevens began to captivate him. "She was lovely, just lovely. Tall and slim, olive-skinned where everyone else around her looked so pale and wan. Hadley had a European elegance," he said, "with the most *perfect* posture of any woman I've ever seen." As soon as he said that I could see the women, myself included, pull our shoulders back and sit up straighter. "She would only wear Chanel No. 5, and even when she left the room, there was a marvelous *sillage* that trailed in her wake—a unique olfactory signature of Chanel, with just the slightest undernotes of fresh hay and horse. Darryl Zanuck once saw her at Scandal and stopped by our table to introduce himself and give her the old, hackneyed line, 'I could make you into a movie star.' Only he really *meant* it. But Hadley just laughed it off. She never married, although she had plenty of offers. Famous Spanish matadors in their little toreador pants would go *mad* for her. But she was devoted to her horses and her dogs, and after her parents died, and her sister was killed, she moved into Casa de las Flores. You'd see her riding along the road on her black Andalusian, Diego. Now *that* was a beautiful animal. Before Rancho Esperanza became the BMW capital of the world, she'd ride Diego to the post office to get the mail. She'd tie up to the hitching post that used to be right in front of Smitty's."

"You're *kidding*?" Nancy said reflexively. "Can you imagine tying a horse up in front of Smitty's? Wouldn't that be fun? To ride your horse to breakfast?"

"She died of cancer much too early. I decided to take over La Casa because I was just afraid if I didn't, the developers would get their hands on her lovely home and turn it into another neo-Tuscan monstrosity."

The narration had a dusty, rehearsed quality, but then Bobby's face positively lit up in spontaneous delight when Fidelia, the cleaning woman he shared with the Berrys, walked into the room carrying a large platter. She was a short, sturdy woman with wide, dependable hips, a round, smiling, copper-colored face, and hair dyed an unflattering shade of red. Although Nancy would've loved having a professional cook, the best she could do was to send Fidelia to adult education for *Easy Hors D'oeuvres* and *Cooking with Wine!*

"You're looking quite fetching this evening, Mrs. Fidelia."

"How are joo, Mr. Bobby?" She seemed genuinely glad to see him.

"Oh, look what you've *done*," he said with obvious pleasure, peering at the platter of grilled asparagus spears wrapped in prosciutto. "Isn't Fidelia just a treasure? I don't think I could live without her."

"How are the boys?" she asked, ignoring the compliment.

"Cute and spoiled as ever."

"You should see these '*boys*,'" Nancy said. "They're *gorgeous* standard poodles."

"Oh, I *love* standards," Cheryl said in her definite way. "Our neighbors in Chilmark have a standard. They're supposed to be *so* smart. And they don't shed, which is a *big* plus as far as I'm concerned. How often do you have to have them groomed?"

"Every three weeks."

"These dogs are perfect," Nancy said "*I* should only look that good."

"I always say, after I die I'd like to come back as my own dog," Bobby said.

"We certainly know about spoiled dogs," Elliot said, turning to Cheryl for corroboration. "My wife makes sure we have two of the most cosseted corgis in the world. The Queen's dogs should only have it this good."

"Yes, Ernie and Larry think *every* dog has an apartment on Park Avenue with a terrace, and a house in Martha's Vineyard for the summer, and a place in Rancho Esperanza where they can run on the beach in January."

"Ernie and Larry. Is that not just too cute?" Nancy said.

"*And* a private plane to get them there," Elliot reminded us.

"I've reconsidered," Bobby Bingham said. "I think I'll come back as *your* dog."

The dinner party, which broke up at ten-thirty, ended on a giddy note when the Kornblatts and the Berrys decided we should all hire a private dance instructor to give us salsa lessons before the Kornblatts left for Cuba in the fall.

"I know someone who's just taken salsa lessons, and I'll get the number of the instructor tomorrow," Nancy promised, as I quickly tried to figure how I'd decline. "And I'm *dying* to see your collection of French drawings," in parting to Bobby Bingham.

I was both relieved and depressed to be alone as I drove home that night. I wondered if I'd made the right decision moving to Rancho Esperanza. There'd been no one in that room I could relate to, except perhaps the maid, who seemed like a nice person. It made me miss Mac. I needed his confirmation to validate the way I was feeling. I wondered what would become of the Berrys if they suddenly found themselves without money. Neither of them had any interest in cooking nor could do anything of real use around the house. Nancy claimed it hurt her back to load the dishwasher and she wouldn't do self-service at the gas station because the fumes made her nauseous. If a toilet ran, Howard depended on the gardener to fix it. Once, when the electricity failed, Howard

became a prisoner on his own property because he couldn't figure out how the gates worked without the remote opener. I remembered what Mac had once said about the Berrys: they were
people who needed to be rich because they just weren't resource-
ful enough to be poor.

On Monday, about the time I'd finally gotten the dinner party
out of my mind, I bumped into Bobby Bingham at the post office.
We'd hardly spoken a word to each other that night, and I wouldn't
have been surprised if he had walked right past me. But not only
did he remember my name, he invited me to his home for tea that
afternoon. I was so taken aback I accepted immediately.

The wisteria Nancy had mentioned was in full and glorious
bloom, its massive vine twisted around the stone pillars of the
front gate and up into the branches of the silvery olive trees. A
gardener blowing leaves off the gravel driveway turned down the
motor and waved as I drove past him up to the house, which sat
at the top of a gentle knoll. I parked in a motor court between
Bobby's classic baby blue Mercedes convertible and a Mitsubishi
Galant with a mangled rear end. From the front door I could turn
and see the sweep of coastline and the yacht club's Monday afternoon sailboat race.

The door to Bobby's house had been left ajar and I stepped
into the foyer, a long gallery hung with portrait paintings, one of
which was a beautiful woman sitting astride a black horse with a
massive arched neck. The vaulted ceiling was decorated with a
Renaissance-style fresco of Cupid and Psyche surrounded by
pretty angels that had real—not Fernando Laguna faux—cracks
in the paint. Two golden cherubs holding candelabras flanked a
carved antique Italian sideboard that stood beneath an Italian
rococo-style gilt wood mirror.

"Bobby?" I called out, and from the direction of the dining
room came the sound of barking. Two black poodles with a silvery

sheen to their coats came toward me, moving a little stiffly on the polished tile floors. I held out my hand in a gesture of peace and after a cursory sniff they yawned and stretched and rubbed their heads against my legs like two big house cats.

With the poodles glued to my side, I peeked into the living room. All the windows were swathed in heavy floral drapery. Every surface was covered with *things*: scrimshaw boxes, tortoiseshell boxes, sterling silver boxes, hatpins, marrow spoons, rugs, leather-bound books, clocks, statuary, paintings—an overwhelming profusion of objects. I felt like I'd stepped back into Rancho Esperanza history. If Hadley Stevens herself had glided into the room with her perfect posture, wearing jodhpurs, riding boots, and Chanel No. 5, I wouldn't have been surprised. But instead, Fidelia appeared in faded leggings and a T-shirt that said CARDOZA'S FISH.

"Boys. Boys," she said to the dogs, "go to Mr. Bobby." Then she turned to me. "Mr. Bobby hiz on the terrace." She opened the French doors off the gallery and motioned for me to follow. Mr. Bobby was in a wrought-iron chair with his back to me, looking up at the mountains.

"Where joo wan I set the table?"

He stood up and I saw he was wearing a silk paisley ascot, cashmere sweatpants, and blue velvet slippers embroidered in gold thread with a Ralph Lauren monogram. "It's such a lovely day, Fidelia. Why don't we sit here underneath the olive trees. But perhaps," he said to me, "you'd like to see my home before we have our champagne. I decided tea was too old-lady-like and I've had enough of that. It's been too long since I've gotten tipsy with a beautiful young woman. Isn't that so, Fidelia?"

"Too long, Mr. Bobby."

He led me through a door into the dining room as Jock and Joe, the dogs, stepped daintily down from the sofa where they'd draped themselves across the pillows and followed us inside, their long nails clicking on the dark wood floors. It was obvious Bobby adored his house. There was so much he wanted to show me—so many bedrooms and bathrooms with their original hand-painted tiles—it took us almost an hour to complete the tour. It wasn't until we returned to the living room, with inlaid mother-of-pearl on the mahogany paneling, that I noticed the small, exquisite drawings placed here and there, most of them on table easels. The first was a Géricault pencil study of two soldiers. Next to it another Géricault pen and ink of a man clutching a horse in water. Then a red chalk drawing on white paper of a man's head.

"Jean-Baptiste Greuze," Bobby said as he saw me looking for the artist's name. "Don't you just love drawings?" he asked, leaning in to examine some Cézanne pen and ink figures. As I walked around the living room there was a charcoal drawing of a mother and child by Renoir, a Corot, a Rodin, a Boucher, and two Matisse simple line drawings of women. "After spending time with my drawings, paintings seem so flashy by comparison. I find I prefer the quiet subtlety of line and tint on paper to the heavy coloration of actual pigment on canvas." I couldn't help but think it was a reference to the Kornblatts and their collection of bright modern art, garish in comparison.

Fidelia had set a table outside with a starched white tablecloth, on which she'd arranged a vase of mauve-pink roses, so large and multipetaled they looked like peonies. A silver champagne bucket and two Baccarat champagne flutes completed the lush still life. Bobby picked up the vase and inhaled the roses, then handed it to me. "You *must* smell these," he said. "They're just divine." He turned in his chair and called to the gardener, who was pruning an olive tree at the far end of the terrace. "Alfonso, we *must* plant more Yves Piaget. Take out the Bewitched. I'm getting bored of their silly pinkness and I detest roses without a scent."

"I think they have some at Wesley Nursery. But not the bare root anymore. It's too late for bare root," the gardener replied. He approached our table for further instructions and I noticed his baseball cap was adorned with fake bird droppings. Although Bobby was keeping up Casa de las Flores in an elegant fashion worthy of Hadley Stevens, evidently he had no control over the sartorial expressions of his help.

"Wesley charges Rancho Esperanza prices," Bobby sniffed, indicating he may have been rich but he wasn't stupid. "See if they have them at the wholesale nursery."

The business of Yves Piaget settled, Bobby focused his attention on the tiny squares of toasted bread, pâté, and caviar with crème fraîche. Jock and Joe looked at Bobby in rapt adoration and they took turns taking these morsels delicately from his fingers. They reminded me of the Berrys courting the Kornblatts for nibbles of the good life.

"At one point in my life," Bobby said, apropos of nothing we'd been talking about, "I thought I wanted to be an artist, but I'm constitutionally incapable of starving in an ugly old garret. I've always needed to be surrounded by beautiful things, beautiful mountains, beautiful trees, beautiful women, beautiful music, and my beautiful dogs. I just can't abide ugliness." He kissed Jock and Joe on the top of their soft, curly heads.

I left Casa de las Flores happily drunk that afternoon. Mr. Bobby had been quaintly genteel, although he was a sought-after companion by the women at Seven Oaks, I suspected he was lonely. I had every intention of inviting him to my house, but I was in the middle of a remodel and my kitchen was torn up. Weeks, then months, then the entire summer went by, and my image of Bobby returned to that of the fussy old snob at the Berrys' dinner party. Once, when I'd spotted him at the post office again, I'd sat in my car until he was safely gone.

Periodically I'd cross paths with Nancy, who'd give me an effusive greeting and then pepper me with a barrage of haute buckshot: ". . . the *next* Yo-Yo Ma" *rat tat tat tat* ". . . the Christo Gates" *rat tat tat tat* ". . . Thomas Friedman, Esa-Pekka, Frank Rich, Tom Stoppard . . . absolutely the *best* crab cakes on the planet" *rat tat tat tat*, before flying off to her massage therapist or a sale at Saks. Then one day she phoned and I could tell from the tone in her voice that this was something different. "Are you still looking for a good maid? Fidelia has a couple of extra days because Bobby Bingham passed away unexpectedly."

I confess, the first thing to cross my mind was "What's going to happen to all that stuff?" Then I thought of the beautiful Yves Piaget roses he'd asked the gardener to plant, and how Bobby would never again delight in their perfume.

"This is so bizarre," Nancy said when I asked her what had happened. "We just saw him at the Chamber Music Society. We ran into him during intermission and he told us his dog was sick and he was going to have to put him down. I knew from Fidelia that he'd put down the other dog a couple weeks before, and so he was *obviously* sad. I mean to lose two dogs in a *month*. But they were both very old. Then two weeks ago Fidelia came in *hysterical* and told us she found Bobby dead in his bed. Apparently, he was just grief-stricken over the dogs and had committed suicide. We'd just *seen* him a few nights before. It's just such a *shock* when something like this happens. I guess he had no heirs. Fidelia told us a lawyer was flying out from New York and they were going to hire an estate liquidator. Fidelia is staying at his house just to watch over everything. She's just *grief*-stricken. I'm sure he's left her something. You know how fond of her he was."

The first day Fidelia came to clean my house, I noticed she was now driving an almost new Toyota. I told her how sorry I was about Mr. Bobby.

"He always say to me, 'Fidelia, I'm going to kill myself when the dogs die,' and I say to him, Mr. Bobby, you no mean it. Why you no marry one of those rich women you go out with? An he say to me, 'Fidelia, I need beauty.' So close yoo eyes, I say to him. But then he kill himself. Why he do such a thing?" she asked as big tears filled her eyes and overflowed down her terra-cotta cheeks.

As Nancy promised, Fidelia turned out to be a good cleaning woman. The only drawback being I was now tethered to the Berrys forever.

"He*l-lo*, it's Nancy. Is Fidelia there today? I have to ask her a quick question. The Kornblatts are coming to town for a week so Elliot can play in the golf tournament at Seven Oaks and I'm giving them a little dinner party next Saturday. I want them to meet Fred and Freyda Ball because Fernando Laguna restored a Rudolph Schindler house they owned in L.A. Do you know Fred and Freyda? Everyone calls them 'the Freds.' They moved here a couple of months ago and we met them in our book club. Fred is a hedge fund manager who apparently does *quite* well—like they fly to Europe on their own Gulfstream Five? Elliot is going to *die* when he finds out the Freds have a G Five. Cheryl and I always make fun of Elliot because he's so plane-conscious. Cheryl calls it plane-us envy. But Elliot has a good sense of humor about it. *Although it doesn't get much bigger than a G Five.* By the way, we bought the French drawings from Bobby Bingham's estate. But before we hang them and have them properly lit, we just want to make sure they're not getting too much light. We may have to put UV coating on the windows because I don't want them to fade. We're having someone from the museum come out and advise us."

"You bought *all* the drawings?" I asked, and from my reaction I'm sure she knew how shocked I was. It just didn't make sense for the Berrys to have acquired such priceless art. It was the Berrys' hobby, if not their life's work, to hunt out a bargain. Since when do fine eighteenth-, nineteenth-, and twentieth-century drawings go on sale?

"We bought everything except for one Renoir. We're going to L.A. this weekend because Howard wants to have them appraised by a dealer who specializes in European drawings. But they'll all be hung by the time everyone gets here. Are you free Saturday?"

I told her I wouldn't be able to make it, having no intention of going through another evening with the Kornblatts. Then I called Fidelia to the phone.

"I wonder," I said as soon as Fidelia hung up, "how did the Berrys get the collection of drawings from Mr. Bobby's estate? Did they buy them directly from the estate liquidator?"

"I sell them to Mr. Howard."

"What do you mean?" I asked, although I knew perfectly well what had happened.

"Mr. Bobby left them to me and I sell them."

"How much did Howard give you?"

"At first Mr. Howard write a check for five thousand dollar and I say to him *no*."

"Five *thousand*?" I was enraged anyone would take advantage of an innocent like Fidelia. It was one thing to cheat Mac and me on a ski vacation, but a poor hardworking maid? What kind of person, what kind of moral lout, does such a thing?

"Then he keep coming back to me until he give me thirty thousand dollars."

"You've got to get the drawings back," I said, already anticipating an ugly fight with Howard and the legal bills I'd be paying on Fidelia's behalf. But would I ever be able to prove Howard had engaged in deception when both parties had agreed on a price?

"I no *wan* them back," she said.

"Didn't Mr. Bobby tell you how *valuable* they were?"

She put down the caddy of cleaning solutions, snapped off her yellow latex gloves, and lay them on the kitchen counter. "Before I work for Mr. Bobby, I work for Señorita Hadley. Mr. Bobby was in love with Señorita Hadley. But I tell him, 'She never marry *you*.' Then Señorita Hadley die from cancer and she leave Mr. Bobby the house so he can take care of Jock and Joe. But when the dogs die, Mr. Bobby, he no haf the house no more. Mr. Bobby always say to me, 'Fidelia, what I do after the dogs die? I no wan to live if I can't live in this house. I can't be poor.' An I say to him, 'Get you self a job.' And he say, 'Fidelia, what can I do? Work at McDonald's?' An I say to him, 'Sell you drawings.' An he say, 'Who wan to buy copies except an *estúpido*?'"

I called Nancy and told her I could come to their dinner party after all. But that night, and for two or three nights after, I couldn't sleep. What kept me awake was my hatred for Howard Berry. I hated him for the way he fawned over the Kornblatts, for how he'd treated Fidelia, ruined my dinner parties, profited from our ski vacation, lied about their stateroom, and pretended to be wealthier than he was. I hated Howard for his puny soul. I rehearsed just what I was going to say to the Berrys at their dinner party, and went over my case against them, justifying what I was about to do. The Berrys were in an untenable position; if the drawings had been genuine, they were guilty of cheating their maid out of millions. But, of course, the drawings were virtually worthless—the creation of a glorified dogsitter. So they were also guilty of passing themselves off as art collectors. What would the Kornblatts—not to mention the Freds—think of the Berrys after I'd revealed the truth?

Bobby Bingham's drawings were hung in the Music Pavilion, beautifully arranged and properly lit with halogen spots. "They come from the Bobby Bingham estate," Nancy announced to all of us. "He used to live in Casa de las Flores. He was a hoot! You remember," she said to the Kornblatts, "but very charming. He was a member of Seven Oaks, and all the older women at the club used to just *drool* over him."

"He was quite a character," Elliot Kornblatt confirmed.

"Did you ever see his house?" Howard turned to the assembly. "He had some phe*nom*enal things. Phe*nom*enal. You can't *imagine* all the things he collected."

"Well, this is pretty amazing right here," Cheryl said in her no-nonsense way.

The Freds marveled over the quality and quantity. Freyda even suggesting Howard might think about joining her on the board of the art museum.

"Of course, you must have gotten them appraised for insurance purposes," I said, stoking the fire.

"We brought them to an art dealer who specializes in European drawings," Howard said.

"They must have been *quite* impressed," Cheryl said. "What did they say?"

"Yes," I repeated. "Tell us what they said," and my heart began to thump and my hands turned to ice. I wished I'd taken a beta-blocker or, at the very least, half a Xanax. But before Howard could answer, Fidelia entered the Music Pavilion with a tray of hors d'oeuvres. There wasn't a moment of discomfort between the Berrys and her. Not a look, not a gesture, nothing. They all pretended beautifully. Fidelia then offered me toasted French bread and a tureen of baked goat cheese with tomato sauce and herbed olives, and Howard refilled my glass with a very nice Pouilly-Fuissé, perfectly chilled. Everything was so pleasant, everyone was in such a good mood; who was I to ruin the evening? I reminded myself what Mac used to say about the Pollois: "You want some kind of justice but you're not going to get it." He was right. What would be gained from telling the truth? Howard would demand his money back from Fidelia and accuse her of fraud, I would be the cause of her unhappiness, she'd most certainly stop working for me, and bumping into the Berrys in years to come would be awkward at best. Besides which, Thanksgiving was coming up, then Christmas, Academy Awards night, the Fourth of July. All the American celebrations I'd more or less taken for granted when I was married were now painfully significant. A woman alone is in no position to be morally righteous.

And so I went on pretending. By the time dessert was served, the Freds had invited the Berrys, the Kornblatts, and me to visit them at the eighteenth-century stone farmhouse they had rented just outside Orvieto. Transportation wasn't mentioned, but I had a feeling it was only a matter of time before the G Five was ours.

Only at the very end of the evening, when I walked into the kitchen to get a glass of water and found Fidelia bent over the sink, did I think to ask the question.

"How come you didn't sell them the chalk drawing of the mother and child? Did you just want a memory of Mr. Bobby?"

"Oh, Mr. Bobby no do *that* one," she said, looking up from a greasy roaster. "The Renoir Mrs. Hadley left to *me*."

The next morning I called the airline and bought a ticket to Jackson Hole, where Mac's family still had his childhood home. Mac's brother had invited me out and I'd made excuses for over a year. But now I needed to go fly-fishing and hiking and kayaking on Jackson Lake in the early morning before the wind comes up— like Mac and I used to do. And when I felt ready, I'd drive out to the cemetery. I wanted to whisper to the grass, "You were right, Mac. You were always so damned right."

The Stud Barn
Lincoln Crowell

Of *course* I know my own name. It's Lincoln Crowell. I know it's Saturday because this was the night of the Englander School fund-raiser, from which I've just come. And I know who's president of the United States—George W. Bush, who has done a great job protecting this country from terrorism, in spite of what the Liberals think. I know all these things, only I can't answer you because the words won't come. You take my pulse and adjust the oxygen mask and all I can do is stare mutely at your young face. But here are the questions I'd like to ask *you*: Why do you wear that silly earring? Is that strip of hair that looks like a furry caterpillar beneath your lower lip supposed to be some kind of fashion statement? Do you think the crouching tiger tattooed on your forearm makes you look like a man? See? I may look elderly and confused, but most of the time there's not a darned thing wrong with my recall *or* my powers of observation. As a matter of fact, my young friend, I can remember things that happened way before you were born. And at this moment, I *prefer* to remember life the way it used to be.

I remember a beautiful, warm day in early October 1956. It happened to be the fifth game of the World Series between the New York Yankees and the Brooklyn Dodgers. A new horse had just arrived at the stud barn. It was a bay Andalusian stallion, a real beauty, and I was getting him settled in. I was listening to the game on the radio when my wife, Chicky, came down to the barn to tell me our daughter was teething and raising quite a fuss.

"I need you to drive to the store and get her some zwieback," she said to me.

"Now?" I said. "Can't it wait until the game is over?"

She insisted it had to be done immediately. The truck at the barn didn't have a radio, so I jumped right in and drove like a bat out of hell so as not to miss the ninth inning. As it turns out I needn't have worried. Because the World Series was coming out of every window of every house, and was playing on every transistor in every yard and broadcasting from every radio of every car I passed. Even the employees in the little Rancho Esperanza Market were gathered around a Bakelite tabletop plugged in at the checkout stand. When the Yankees clinched the game 2–0, I was at the corner of Star Pine Hill and Vista del Mar and you could hear a cheer up and down the streets and all through Rancho Esperanza and across the entire nation from coast to coast. Because we all knew that Don Larsen had just done what no player had ever done before in a World Series. He had pitched a perfect game. And no one has ever beaten his record.

That's what I want to tell you, my young friend with the earring and tattoo—the way life was back then. You had *real* heroes and the entire country rooted for them because they were *our* heroes. You didn't have a big, angry Barry Bonds all hyped-up on steroids, going around with an up-yours attitude. You didn't have all these drugged out rehab celebrities having children out of wedlock with this person and then that person. You had honest athletes and glamorous movie stars and wholesome pastimes. You had children who respected adults and adults who didn't behave like children. That's the America I grew up in.

And let me tell you, my boy, about my family's ranch down in Temecula, where we grew avocados and Valencia oranges. In the spring and fall, the smell of orange blossoms would just about knock your socks off. You'd open up your bedroom window at night and the whole room smelled like perfume. We might not have had the biggest ranch in Temecula, but we did okay. And back then, when you could get a whole meal of turkey, mashed potatoes with gravy, green beans, and apple pie for twenty-five cents, "okay" was all you needed to be. That was also the America I knew.

I'm a patriot and I make no apologies for it. When I was eighteen I was already an aviation cadet getting set to defend my country. That was 1942. Right after the war began. Only a year earlier, I had just started at USC. There used to be an old-time actor at Warner Bros. named Wayne Morris, and he played leading men and action-type heroes. Well, he was a member of the U.S. Naval Reserve and he came to campus one day. At that time they had the V-5 program where college students, like myself, could go into the naval flight-training program. If you got accepted, you could be trained as a naval or marine aviator. That sounded great to me so I signed up right after Pearl Harbor. I went through preflight, primary, and advanced training, and then I graduated. And when you graduated from that program, if you were in the top 10 percent of your class, you had the option of applying to the Marine Corps. I wanted to be a fighter pilot. That was my designation. We were down at Miramar Air Station in San Diego, and we had all our medical shots, and we were all packed, and our gear was all stowed, and we were headed for the South Pacific. I went to bed that night thinking I was shipping out. But when I got up the next morning, I saw they'd posted something on the bulletin board. There were sixteen names out of about sixty guys, and I was one of them. I got reassigned to El Toro Marine Air Base, down by Santa Ana in Orange County. They reassigned me to the Naval Air Transport Service. My job was to ferry planes all over the country. I'd go to Seattle and pick up a Corsair and take it to New York. I'd be in New York and they'd say to me, "Take this dive bomber to Chicago." Or Walla Walla, Washington, or wherever they needed it. I flew all kinds of planes. No one ever showed me how. I just did it. I'd get in, look around for about five minutes to figure out where everything was, and then take off into the sky. I was nineteen years old and had an airline priority higher than any general, congressman, or senator. The only person who could kick me off an airplane was a member of the U.S. Cabinet. What do you think of that, my boy?

Of course, I was very disappointed I didn't get to go overseas. *You'd* probably think, "Didn't you ever worry about dying overseas—weren't you relieved to stay home?" And I'd say to you, "I always regretted it. I wanted to be with my buddies. I tried to transfer but they said forget it. You can't go. You have to stay here."

But we had a good time at home, better than you'd ever imagine. There was good camaraderie. And not only that, we had our pick of the girls. That's how I first came to Rancho Esperanza. I was dating this gal named Delilah who looked just like Rita Hayworth—red hair, beautiful figure—and she lived here. Back then Rancho Esperanza was just this wonderland. I couldn't believe people actually lived like that. I'll never forget—Delilah took me to a party at Casa de las Flores, owned by the Stevenses of St. Louis. Delilah had gone to high school with Mercie and Hadley, whose parents owned the estate. They were the famous Stevens sisters. Mercie Stevens was blond and vivacious and just as pretty as a picture, but, unfortunately, she died quite young in a skiing accident. Hadley Stevens had more of a Mediterranean look about her and was a lot of fun, too. She was an attractive gal—not nearly as pretty as her sister—but a super horsewoman. Years later, I gave her Diego, my black Andalusian.

Mrs. Stevens was a society type who'd built a music pavilion on the property where she put on entertainment. The women dressed in evening gowns and long gloves, and the men came in their tuxes. It was just a beautiful sight, let me tell you. As opposed to the way people dress today. I just went to a funeral where the grandson of the man who died kept his baseball cap on throughout the whole service. What kind of respect does that show? Back then, people knew how to dress for the occasion and everyone felt good doing it. It wasn't a hardship to put on a tux. The night I was there, Mario Lanza sang. He was just this young, good-looking Italian kid—maybe twenty-one or twenty-two—with a smooth tenor voice. That was before all the operas and radio recordings and his movie career. No one had ever heard of him except Mrs. Stevens, who had seen him sing at his debut back east. Then, of course, after the war, Mario Lanza became a household name.

Mrs. Stevens had invited all kinds of people to the pavilion that night, including Charles Lindbergh. Do you even know who Charles Lindbergh is? Well, I'll tell you. He had once been my hero. You have to hand it to the old gal, Mrs. Stevens. She didn't let his Nazi-loving politics get in the way of friendship. As far as I was concerned, Lindbergh was just a crum-bum. He may have been a great aviator but he was no patriot. I felt he got what he deserved when he was denied reinstatement into the Air Corps after we entered the war. He later redeemed himself by flying combat missions in the South Pacific, but I never felt the same way about him.

The night Mario Lanza sang was also the first time I saw Chicky. Chicky was just a young girl then, and she was there with her parents. In those days, parents and children spent time together socially. The kids didn't just go up to their rooms and do drugs and hang out with their friends. The generations mixed. Chicky and I met up again a few years later, and that's when we started dating and fell in love.

Chicky's family came from Pasadena, and when Pasadena became too hot in the summer, they would move everyone, including the servants, dogs, and horses, to their place in Rancho Esperanza. And what a place it was, young man, what a place it was. If you looked in one direction, you saw the Pacific. And if you turned your head in the other, why, you had an almost 180-degree view of the mountains. It had a redwood grove, the largest one south of Santa Cruz, and a meadow, which in the spring was a colored carpet of lupine, Indian paintbrush, and poppies. The Indians thought it was sacred ground and built their village there. Then the Spanish got hold of it. The old Stokes estate where I lived was once part of a three-thousand-acre parcel given by the Spanish government to a Captain José Dominguez. He named it after his wife, Esperanza, and eventually Rancho Esperanza became the name of the whole town we live in today. It was in that meadow—where the Indians once prospered and the vaqueros galloped their horses—that I married Chicky Stokes, June 27, 1953. Chicky's mother had arranged the wedding to her liking and made sure it got written up, not only in the *Rancho Gazette* and the *Pasadena Star-News* but the *San Francisco Chronicle* and the *New York Times*.

Chicky's mother was a force of nature, let me tell you. Everything had to be just so. She'd walk around her house with a feather duster waking up the cats because she didn't approve of them sleeping during the day. She always wore a hat when she went out, and the milliner at I. Magnin knew to call when a particularly nice one came in to the store. When she'd walk into Scandal, the bartender would drop what he was doing to make her martini, which she'd drink with her white gloves on. She was a hell of a horsewoman, too. She rode western until she got pregnant with Chicky, then changed to English so her belly wouldn't hit the horn of the saddle. She was out fox hunting five days before giving birth. I always said that if Chicky's mother had been supreme commander of the Allied forces in Europe, Hitler would have run the other way. Chicky's mother died not long after we were married. At her funeral, all her hats were displayed on the pews in the back of the church, and her friends were invited to take one home to remember her by. After Chicky's father passed on, Chicky and I moved into the big house and lived there for over forty years. Until we sold it. And I can say without a doubt, those were the days of heaven.

Then there was the day of hell. Today. Saturday for your information. The Englander School's *A Thousand and One Arabian Nights* fund-raiser at the old Stokes estate. How can I explain what it was like returning to my old home again? How can I convey how angry I felt when I saw what they'd done to the place? I don't know why I even went. I usually try to avoid these charity events. Chicky and I get invitations in the mail—four and five of them a week—and most of them end up right in the trash. But my granddaughter attends Englander and my daughter, Claire, had bought four tickets at $125 a pop, hoping her mother and I would accompany her. But Chicky had flat out refused to go. She didn't want to go back to the old house or meet the new people. She'd heard, through the grapevine, they were real Hollywood types and that they'd practically taken the old place down to the studs when they remodeled it, which just didn't sit well with her *at all*. I didn't want to go either but I also couldn't disappoint my daughter. I said to Claire, "I'll go with you but I'm not wearing a costume, for heaven's sake. I'm eighty-two years old and I'm not dressing up like Rudolph Valentino. I'll put on a tie and jacket and that will just have to do."

This Italian fellow who bought the place, Vincent Rizzo's his name, was dressed like a sultan, with a big fake jewel in the center of his white turban, and it just annoyed me the way he strutted around like one of our old peacocks. You could just tell he liked himself too much. His wife was all decked out in a harem costume and looked like an X-rated version of that gal in *I Dream of Jeannie*. I didn't want to stare, but you couldn't help it. She had on these royal purple chiffon harem pants worn very low—way south of her belly button—and a top that left little to the imagination. It wasn't any more than a bra made out of brass coins or something. And she was stacked. She was one sexy gal, which I can still appreciate, believe it or not, my young friend. But I didn't think her outfit was appropriate for an Englander School fund-raiser.

There were probably over two hundred people there, but I didn't know a soul except Sally and Walter Topping. The last time I'd seen them was at their thirtieth wedding anniversary celebration at the Rancho Esperanza Country Club. Sally's just a peach of a gal and her father and I went way back because he was the Methodist minister in town. He was a real nice fellow and a scratch golfer. Walter runs the Rancho Esperanza Savings and Loan and is very community-minded. He's maybe twenty-five years my junior, but we've worked on a few things together and I always found him to be a can-do kind of guy. At first glance I didn't even recognize him. He was dressed like Yasir Arafat with one of those black-and-white kerchiefs on his head. He'd even grown some stubble.

"Hey young fella," he said to me. "You're the smartest one here tonight, coming in a tie and jacket. I don't like these costume events myself."

He was just being diplomatic because I was the only person not dressed like I was still living in the Ottoman Empire. Even the serving people were dressed like genies and they kept coming up to me with fried balls of mashed chickpeas on skewers, or something like that, and all kinds of garlicky dips that play havoc with my acid reflux.

"I think it's fun every once in a while to put on a costume," Sally said. "Some of these people are just so *creative*."

Well, I didn't want to tell her I thought the whole thing was just stupid. Sally is one of the dearest women and I didn't see any point in bursting her bubble. Other than Walter and Sally, there was no one I knew to talk to. There was a wrangler who'd trucked his Arabian over from Santa Lucia. He'd been hired to do some kind of show with the horse, so I went up to him and we passed the time. The horse was a pretty little filly but I never much cared for Arabians. Too small and too hot.

You have no idea how awful the whole evening was. There was a giant tent set up on the lawn, and inside were fancy chandeliers and Persian carpets. We all had to sit on the floor on pillows and eat lamb and rice with our fingers. Everyone around me was saying, "Isn't this great? Isn't this fun?" And I thought to myself, "*This* is your idea of fun? Sitting on the ground like a bunch of Bedouins?" Maybe for people thirty years old who haven't had hip replacement surgery, but I've never been so uncomfortable in my entire life. It just made me long for the old days in Rancho Esperanza and the kinds of parties *we* used to have at the house. We didn't need all the fuss and costumes to have fun. And we didn't have to hire horses, either, because we had a barn full of the most beautiful Andalusians in the whole country.

Every Fourth of July all the neighbors were invited; we usually had over a hundred people back then. We gave it down at the stud barn and set up the bar underneath the big oak trees so there was always plenty of shade. We brought out the picnic tables and Chicky did them up with red-checkered tablecloths and the blue-and-white tin plates, her "campfire dishes" she used to call them. And in the center of the tables she'd put good old American daisies in mason jars. We'd hire Clancy Boyd to do the cooking, he'd bring in one of those big grills and fire it up with oak and apple wood, and everyone would fill their plates with ribs and tri-tip, and he made a damn good coleslaw and beans. And when the sun went down, we'd build a fire in the pit and people would sit around on hay bales, and those of us who had a guitar or banjo or harmonica would play. Those are the kinds of neighbors we had back then and everyone had a marvelous time.

And you could *talk* at those parties. What's the point of having a party if you can't talk to people? At this *A Thousand and One Arabian Nights* extravaganza, everyone was shouting over the music. They'd hired some DJ, some kid about your age, and he had these speakers about as big as VW Bugs. I don't understand why music has to be so loud at these events. And why would someone pick a kid to choose the music? Why don't they have an adult with some taste? In the thirties and forties, we had the great romantic composers, and great witty composers like Cole Porter and Noël Coward—all the great standards came from them. In the swing era we had the big bands and boy, did we have great musicians—Louis Armstrong, Artie Shaw. I love Tommy Dorsey, Glenn Miller, Benny Goodman. Those were wonderful bands in those days and that's the kind of music we played for people. And so many great singers—Billie and Ella, Sinatra and Crosby. It was a time of so much talent. As compared with what they call talent today. I listened to the music at this party tonight and I couldn't understand a word they were saying. They were singing a song and I just looked at my daughter and said, "Do you understand what they're saying, because I don't understand one single word. I know I'm getting a little deaf but the music has no melody to it." There was this one song, I don't remember what it was, but it went something like, *I love you no more, I love you no more, I love you no more.* This went on and on. Twenty-eight times they're saying the same thing over and over again. And those rappers. Forget it. Music to me has to have a melody. If there's no melody, I don't care what kind of song it is, it's not a song.

Then my son-in-law piped up about how I should keep an open mind and I should just *listen* to what they're trying to say.

"You mean like those black comedians you listen to?" I said. "Like that crum-bum who did the Academy Awards a few years ago? To call him a comedian is pushing the envelope. He's just a foul mouth."

"But he's funny," Nacho said. "Have you ever really watched his act?"

"I watched him," I said. "He can't say a sentence without three 'fucks' in it. Why would they want to have a person like that represent the motion picture industry in front of the whole world?"

"So who do *you* think is funny?" Nacho said, in his superior way that just drives me nuts.

"I'll tell you who I think is funny. Jack Benny and George Burns and Gracie Allen and Buddy Hackett doing the Chinese waiter routine. Maybe it's not politically correct today, but by god, it was funny. Today you can say 'fuck' and 'suck' and all those words, but you can't have a Chinese waiter in your routine because you'll *offend* someone. But this black kid offends *everyone.* This is supposed to represent America? Just like when Pepsi-Cola decided they were going to hire this Snoop Doggie, whatever his name is. They couldn't believe how much their sales fell off. People just don't like this kind of thing. It may be very Hollywood, and very hip, and very New Yorky, but it ain't red America."

When the belly dancer came out and tried to get me to stand up and wiggle my hips like a fool, I excused myself and went inside to find a bathroom. Vincent Rizzo was standing in the hallway that led to our old dining room. It used to have beautiful mahogany paneling and we had English prints of horses and hounds. But they took out all that beautiful wood and now everything is white. Bright white. And there were these large "conceptual sketches" on the walls, maybe four or five of them, done by this guy Christo. The "artiste" who did those orange rags, something like two thousand of them, hanging on poles in Central Park. Vincent Rizzo was showing these drawings to a woman who came up to me like we were long-lost friends. I'd never seen her before in my life but I knew the name—Freyda Ball. She and her husband, Fred, are real L.A. types who moved here and immediately started throwing their money around. The Englander School now has the Ball Theater courtesy of you know who. Freyda Ball was laughing and flirting with Vince Rizzo and even turned her charms on me, if you can call them charms. In my opinion, she was a little long in the tooth to be behaving like a femme fatale. She started going on and on about how she went to New York to see the Christo "installation" and how *exciting* it was to see the color orange in *February* and how it stuck out against the gray and made her appreciate the this and the that. And I wanted to say to her, what does an orange blanket have to do with anything? Why do you think that's art? People would rather look at the park. It's pretty in the park, you've got trees, you've got a lake, you've got ducks. Now, because of this guy, you have to look at big orange handkerchiefs.

Then Vincent invited us into the dining room to show us his "newest acquisition." On the left side, where we had the sideboard and all those beautiful dog plates, there was now a painting. I would say it was maybe ten feet long and went from the floor to the ceiling. Another one of those contemporary artists. But this painting was totally white. White as snow. And in the bottom right-hand corner was a big red blob, and Freyda Ball is standing in front of it saying Oooh! Oooh! You could just tell she was "The Emperor's New Clothes" kind of liberal who thinks something is great because she reads some critic who *tells* her it's great. And I'm standing there thinking, that's the dumbest thing I've ever seen in my whole life. I mean, why do people equate *that* with art? That's not art. That's somebody pulling the wool over your eyes and *telling* you it's art. When I look at the Old Masters and even some more contemporary ones, there's beautiful line, beautiful feeling. Chicky's parents collected English oil paintings of dogs. Some of them are hundreds of years old, but they're timeless. You look at the eyes of some of these animals and they're so lifelike. I wouldn't try to define art for anybody. Everybody has a different feeling about it. But I find all this modern abstract stuff just plain phony. People are being pretentious by saying, "That's art, and you really have to under*stand* art to understand this because this has such hidden *meaning* because the white represents blah blah blah and the red something else." I'll tell you what it is. It's a white canvas with a big splotch of red in the corner of it. That's what it is. And don't tell me that it relieves the inner self or whatever they try to make of it.

I finally made it to the bathroom to relieve *my* inner self and when I came out, I knew I needed to walk down to the old stud barn. I needed to get my grounding. There's nothing like the smell of hay and horses. Horses just get into your blood and their warm breath in your face sets your mind straight. I didn't even know if there were any horses left on the property—except for the hired Arabian. But I figured it was worth a shot. Anything was better than standing there listening to Vincent Rizzo go on and on about his "acquisition."

It's a ways down to the barn, which is why we always kept the John Deere handy. But it was a nice night and I figured, if nothing else, the walk would do me good. Clear my mind. But the night-blooming jasmine and *Pittosporum* were so potent they made my head swim. And the frogs and the crickets by the pond were raising a ruckus that even *I* could hear. I remembered all the nights I'd bed down on the sleeping porch under the German eiderdown comforter we got as a wedding gift and I'd drift off to sleep listening to that racket. I thought of the deer that used to live in the redwood grove before most of it was subdivided and developed. Chicky and I would watch them come out in the evening to drink at the pond. I wondered where they'd all gone. I passed the gardener's cottage and thought of the Danish cook who had lived there with her son. Chicky and I treated that boy almost as a son ourselves. I put him on his first horse. And he learned how to play tennis with my daughter, Claire. All of these happy, pleasant memories passed through my mind and I was feeling almost young again.

When I reached the old stud barn there was no smell of hay or horses. The riding arena and corrals were all gone and the drinking troughs had been planted with flowers. The barn doors were ajar, a light was on, and so I stepped inside. Where my stallions once whinnied and snorted and ejaculated there were now office chairs with lumbar supports and computer screens swimming with tropical fish. We used to have chalkboards with feeding instructions at each stall but now there were movie posters on the walls— movies our esteemed host had, apparently, produced. They were the kind of movies with real he-man types—guys with big muscles and machine guns and fighter planes—about as opposite from Vincent Rizzo as you could get. The dirt floor, which had been raked daily by our groom, Ramón, was now covered with wide planked wood flooring and cowhide rugs. The only reminder that it was once a working barn was the old western saddles used as decoration. But that wasn't the most surprising thing. Not by a long shot, my boy. It was what I spotted across the room—something on the floor that caught my eye. At first I thought I must be mistaken, my eyes playing tricks. So I walked over to see what it was. And lying on that creamy cowhide rug were the purple chiffon harem pants. Yes! It was true! Then I heard the sound—a woman in the thralls of ecstasy. Although it's been a while, it's not a sound you easily forget. My heart began to race in my chest as I walked right up to Diego's old stall. And there was a sight I'll never forget as long as I live. Walter Topping had mounted the beautiful and exotic Mrs. Vincent Rizzo. The coins on her bra had caught the light and, as he pounded away, a thousand shimmering Tinkerbells danced on the walls and tin roof in an orgiastic frenzy. I turned around and ran out of that barn like the thief of Baghdad.

By the time I reached the house my leg and arm felt completely numb. Sally Topping was outside looking for Walter and when she saw me staggering around like a drunkard, she ran up to help. "Dear sweet Sally," I wanted to say. But my lips and tongue and voice wouldn't make the sounds.

So here I am, my young, tattooed friend, connected to oxygen and monitors and things that go beep in the night. Good Lord, deliver us! And this is what I know for sure: I am an old man now. There will be no more Scheherazades, with their soft skin and warm sweet breath. There are just Freyda Balls with horse teeth and sagging breasts. There is Chicky who stopped thinking about it years ago. And there is Death, waiting for me with open legs.

The Shoe Girl at Magnin's
Renee Green

About a year ago my husband Jerry and I were going through a very stressful situation and I was afraid I was going to make myself sick. My internist, who also practices alternative medicine, said he'd teach me how to meditate. I was supposed to lie on his couch and close my eyes and think of a place that made me feel happy and relaxed. "It could be a hammock by a lake," he suggested, "or a meadow filled with flowers or a sunset at the beach." But when I closed my eyes and tried to recall a place that made me feel really happy, the only image that came to mind was the ladies' room at I. Magnin.

Magnin's was where my mother and I always went right after my orthodontist appointment. Dr. Zuckerman's office was in Beverly Hills on Santa Monica, and as we left his building and headed toward Wilshire, I could already see I. Magnin from blocks away. It was built in the Art Deco style and sheathed in white Carrara marble that gleamed in the sun like the Taj Mahal, without the crypt and turrets. The ground floor sparkled with crystal chandeliers and they had the best perfume and cosmetics department in the city. But the ladies' room on the second floor was the most elegant room I'd ever seen; black-and-white checkerboard marble floors, black enamel sinks on sleek chrome legs, and dressing tables with black marble tops and little white upholstered chairs. But the best thing was the fully enclosed private stalls, with full-length beveled mirrored doors and little silver knobs you could turn to read OCCUPIED. I grew up in a very middle-class household with one bathroom we all shared, so this was the height of luxury. There were even folded white hand towels, and lotion dispensers with the most wonderful smelling hand cream. Everywhere you turned were mirrors and reflections. It looked like a 1930s movie set where Fred Astaire and Ginger Rogers would come dancing in. He'd be in a tux and she'd be wearing a white satin gown cut on the bias, an ermine shrug, and a nice, fat diamond bracelet. The ladies' room at I. Magnin made me feel glamorous. Or as glamorous as a twelve-year-old with braces can feel.

I. Magnin was the kind of store that catered to "ladies" who could afford understated, well-made clothes. Even though I was young, and my family didn't have a lot of money, I already loved the feel of cashmere and silk charmeuse and the way a crisp pleat hung on a good wool skirt. When I got my first job out of college and made ninety-five dollars a week as a receptionist for an advertising firm, I'd save my money and go to I. Magnin for that one beautiful scarf, or the leather belt that could make an outfit. I remember my mother saying, "If you want to be one of those ladies who shop at I. Magnin, you better make sure you marry well."

When Jerry and I moved to Rancho Esperanza eighteen years ago, the little I. Magnin on Ocean Avenue was not only a place to shop, but also a place to go whenever I felt homesick. I spent a lot of time at Magnin's and it was there, in the shoe department, I first met Delilah Porter. I was holding a brown suede high-heeled shoe, deciding if I wanted to try it on, when I sensed someone standing behind me. I smelled her perfume before I actually saw her. It was an old-fashioned rose scent. I turned, ready to inform whoever was hovering that I was still looking, thank you, and saw an older woman, dressed in a black wool bouclé suit, the skirt just grazing the bottom of her knee. Around her neck was a strand of tiny cultured pearls and on her pinkie finger was a small gold ring like a child would wear.

Everything about her was so understated and prim. Except for two things: the first was her name. You think of Delilah as a vixen, a seductress, and the ultimate betrayer of men. Delilah Porter looked like she still might be a virgin. The second was her hair. It was a deep shade of red, with outrageous, brassy highlights— a result of oxidation and too many years of do-it-yourself Miss Clairol. It was worn in a wavy pageboy, which I found out years later was tortured into place with Dippity-do and little rollers wound tight as a spool of thread. She was from another time—a type of saleswoman from my childhood. She made me feel like I was a little girl again, shopping in I. Magnin with my mother.

"Aren't those looove-ly?" She spoke in a soft, ladylike voice, almost as if she were talking to herself. "Such a well-made shoe. I just love the way Bruno Magli fits the foot. Even their high heels are a pleasure to wear. I've had some of my Bruno Maglis for over twenty years."

It was definitely a sales pitch, but done in such a genteel and persuasive manner, who wouldn't want to try them on? After walking around the shoe department, looking at them in the mir- ror, and discussing the shoes' merits with Delilah, who seemed to really know and love her merchandise, she convinced me that I could hardly afford *not* to own these wonders of cobblery. "May I put this on your I. Magnin charge?" she asked, and when I dug in my purse and found my card, she leaned in closer. "If you give me your phone number," she said in a hushed and confidential voice, "I'll let you know when we're having our pre-sale." From then on, whenever I went shopping for shoes, I made sure Delilah was my salesgirl.

Like I. Magnin itself, Delilah was a reassuring fixture, always dressed in a black or navy blue dress or suit, with her string of tiny pearls and a gentle smile that reminded me of a martyred saint. Just being around her mild-mannered, even-tempered way relaxed me, and even when I wasn't shopping for shoes I found myself stopping by her department. But I wondered about Delilah. I. Magnin was one thing, but she seemed too innocent and gentle to cope in the *real* world. How would she handle a crooked car mechanic or some idiot repairman who came on a rainy day and didn't think to take off his shoes before muddying her floors? Did people take advantage of her meek nature, or did she have someone who protected her best interests? She wore no wedding ring. Had she ever been married? Was she a widow left with no money? Is that why she still worked at an age when most women in Rancho Esperanza were playing golf and enjoying their grandchildren? What was her story?

Delilah wasn't much of a conversationalist. She seemed to be enamored of Old Money and liked to talk about the history of Rancho Esperanza—"It used to be a place where wealthy Easterners would send their misfit children because it was so much further away than Palm Beach or Southampton." But the only personal history she'd volunteered was that she was born in Rancho Esperanza, and had lived there most of her life.

"Oh, I just couldn't *imagine* living anywhere else. I left it once, but realized this is where I belong."

Another time we were discussing restaurants in town and she said she hardly ever ate out. "When I was growing up, there was a restaurant called Scandal. It was in an old Victorian building and that's where all the best people in town used to eat. In those days the men were required to wear jackets and there was a hand-painted plaque by the front door for women that said, NO SLACKS PLEASE. Even Katharine Hepburn was turned away for lunch, but she returned that evening in formal attire. You'd see Rolls Royces parked out front as well as pickup trucks the ranchers drove. It was said that Scandal got its name because it used to be a house of . . . ill repute."

Of course, "ill repute" was said in a whisper. She was a relic of old Rancho Esperanza, a vanishing breed, a piece of living history. They weren't making them like Delilah Porter anymore—if they ever made them like her in the first place. She was a mystery to me and I couldn't imagine what she did when she wasn't in one of her tailored dark suits padding around the shoe department of Magnin's in smart but sensible footwear. But Rancho Esperanza is a very small town and I didn't have to wait too long to find out.

On a Sunday morning, about a year after I'd first met her, Jerry and I were going for a hike with our dog, Sparky, when we spotted an old model Karmann Ghia parked at the trailhead. The rear door was open and Delilah Porter was leaning in, one knee on the upholstery, retrieving something from the backseat. When she emerged from the car and straightened up, she had a large, heavy pair of binoculars around her neck, and a paperback of *Western Birds* in her hand on which she had put a clear plastic sleeve to protect the cover. Of course, I thought. A birdwatcher. How perfectly Delilah. She was in walking shorts worn, I shudder to say, with pantyhose, and her blue oxford shirt was crisply ironed. A straw hat with a chinstrap protected her pale skin. The navy blue Keds on her small feet seemed girlish. I noticed her legs, which had always been covered by a modest hem, were actually quite shapely.

"Isn't it just a glorious day," she said, not looking at Jerry, who was standing beside me. After agreeing that the weather was glorious, I asked how the birdwatching was going.

"I've had a very exciting morning. I spotted an eastern phoebe. What would an eastern phoebe be doing *here*?"

Out of anyone else's mouth it would have sounded like a joke, but Delilah was incapable of humor. Having no idea about the bird's faulty sense of direction, I introduced her to Jerry and the dog. She finally looked at Jerry and smiled. "Your store is just a *joy* to be in. So tastefully done."

"What were you doing in my store?" Jerry owns a men's clothing store in town, and Delilah didn't exactly fit the profile of his typical customer.

"Bobby Bingham brought me," she said with pride in her voice, as if she had snagged the star football player to take her to the prom. "Bobby has marvelous taste and so *appreciates* the *quality* of your merchandise."

"Bobby Bingham only buys on sale," Jerry said after she'd gone off, "and he always struck me as being gay."

For whatever reason, that little encounter at the trailhead was the turning point in our relationship. The very next time I went to Magnin's, Delilah intercepted me in the cosmetics department. She looked tired, even thinner than usual, and I asked if she was feeling all right. That's when she told me about Mrs. Finley.

"I share a house with a woman I've known for many years, but unfortunately she's an alcoholic and the situation is going from bad to worse. She can be very abusive at times. She's on medication and if she's drinking, she'll just forget to take her pills. Also there's an Abyssinian cat I'm very fond of, and sometimes I think the poor thing would starve to death if I wasn't there to open a can of food. When Mrs. Finley is drinking sometimes she forgets to feed *herself*. I'm just afraid she'll burn down the house if I'm not there to make sure the toaster oven is off. I unplug it every time I use it, and hide it under the counter where she's too lazy to look for it."

Okay, I thought. Now at least I know where Delilah lives. But from then on, every time I bumped into her—at the market, the post office, the pharmacy—I heard about Mrs. Finley, whose behavior became increasingly erratic. Mrs. Finley threw a telephone at Delilah. Mrs. Finley fell in the tub and Delilah had to get her out. Mrs. Finley was smoking in bed again.

The more I heard, the more I wondered how Delilah—a well-spoken, fastidious woman—had ended up living with a sloppy and abusive alcoholic. It occurred to me that maybe Delilah's life was so bland and limited that Mrs. Finley added drama and excitement. Or Delilah's life was so empty of love, anything was better than nothing. Whatever the reason, her situation made me feel a little guilty at how easy my life was. How fortunate I was to have a husband, family, and income that allowed me to live where I wanted, and with whom. I felt I had to do something to help her, and began by urging Delilah to find a new place.

"I wish I could move, but I don't think Mrs. Finley would ever get a tenant who'd put up with her. Goodness knows her daughter is no help. All she wants is her mother's money. It's really quite sad."

About a year after I'd first heard of Mrs. Finley, she died of congestive heart failure. Delilah had kept me informed throughout the whole ordeal. Now that her landlady was finally gone, I thought Delilah's life might improve. But Mrs. Finley's daughter turned out to be as unappreciative of Delilah as her mother had been.

"She's just a nightmare," Delilah told me in her composed voice. "She never came by to see her mother without asking for money, and now that her mother is dead she wants me out in two weeks so she can sell the house. Oh, dear. What a nuisance."

"What are you going to do?"

"I wish I knew. That daughter of hers would like to see me thrown out in the street," she said with as much emotion as if she were talking about a zipper that had gotten stuck.

For a while it looked like Delilah might just have predicted her own fate; one apartment was too expensive, one place didn't allow animals—she had inherited Mrs. Finley's cat, Mr. Jingles—one place was too close to the freeway, one house had mold that affected her as soon as she walked in the front door, one place was nice but too far from work. I ended up calling anyone I knew who might know of a place that wasn't too expensive. I described Delilah as the perfect tenant—quiet, neat, single, and older. When I mentioned her to our neighbor, Sally, she added a piece to the Delilah puzzle.

"Oh, poor Delilah," Sally said. "Mother used to talk about her. She was supposed to have been one of the most beautiful girls in Rancho Esperanza. Mother said she had the most luxurious red hair, just like Rita Hayworth. Her family was Nazarene, and the Nazarenes don't allow drinking or movies or dancing. Even though Daddy was the Methodist minister in town, I don't think they considered us *real* Christians. They thought we were all just going to the Devil for being so theologically liberal. So Mother and Daddy didn't socialize with them, even though we were neighbors. Apparently, one night Delilah got into an argument with her father. Maybe she came home late, or he caught her drinking. She was in college so she could have been out with friends he didn't approve of—we never knew for sure. Whatever it was, to punish her he cut off all her beautiful hair. She ran out of the house and tried to commit suicide by driving his car right off Palisades Drive. Can you imagine doing that to your child? After that, she disappeared for about ten years. No one knows where she went or what happened to her. Mother thinks she may have had a nervous breakdown. When she finally came back to Rancho Esperanza, her father was dead, her brother was living back east, and she was left to take care of the mother. When her mother died she went to work at I. Magnin in the shoe department, and that's where she's been ever since. Poor thing. What a waste. It was child abuse what that father did to her. He ruined her life."

The story about that disgusting piece of crap father cutting off all her beautiful red hair was so revolting I couldn't get it out of my mind. No wonder Delilah could hardly look at Jerry. No wonder she'd never gotten married and dated Bobby Bingham. No wonder she worked in the *women's* shoe department. She hated men, and for a good reason.

At the final hour, as Delilah was about to be tossed on the street by Mrs. Finley's greedy daughter, Delilah landed on her feet like the Abyssinian. She moved into a charming guest cottage on a shady private lane. Delilah invited me over one afternoon for Twinings Prince of Wales Tea. Two gay men owned the main house, an older ranch style decorated in heavy Asian motif, with an array of Chinatown tchotchkes and refrigerator magnets that dispelled the notion that all gay men have good taste. A small garden surrounded Delilah's cottage and she'd planted honeysuckle and marigolds to attract the birds. The rent was too expensive for her income, but she loved her little cottage and doted on Jay and Leo, her landlords. And they, apparently, adored her.

As I had predicted, Delilah was the perfect tenant—smart, responsible, and honest. When her landlords were away, she took care of their cocker spaniels and watered the houseplants. One winter during the heavy rains, when Jay and Leo were at a hair show in Las Vegas, she saved their house from flooding by calling the Department of Water and Power to clear the street drains clogged with debris. When their dogs got into rat poison due to a neighbor's carelessness, she got them into her little Karmann Ghia and rushed them to the vet. She told me all this, and described the candlelit dinners they had—Leo loved to cook—and that sometimes Bobby Bingham joined the festivities. Three gay men suited Delilah perfectly. For the next couple years or so, all seemed well. Until I. Magnin announced they were closing.

It was a surprise to all of us but especially to Delilah. In spite of her retail experience no jobs were available, especially for a woman her age. Poor Delilah. Her gabardine suits were getting shiny from too many pressings, her Karmann Ghia was beginning to rust, and I realized she was probably telling the truth when she'd said some of her shoes were over twenty years old. The surprising thing was Jay and Leo were very unsympathetic and refused to adjust her rent.

"You know, they owe money to just about *everyone*," she informed me in her even-tempered way. "I've paid for things out of my own pocket, and I know I'll never get reimbursed. I wouldn't be surprised if they declared bankruptcy before their creditors get wise. And Leo is a gambler. Every time they go to Las Vegas, Jay has to practically *drag* Leo away from the slot machines. He has an addictive personality. He's put on weight and just keeps getting heavier and heavier. I've offered to do the housekeeping for a reduction in rent, but they're just *implacable*."

Again Delilah looked for a place to live. But rents had gone up considerably since the last time she was without a home.

"Why don't you live with Bobby Bingham?" I suggested. She'd told me time and again how large his house was, how tastefully it was decorated, and how much she enjoyed his company.

"Oh, that would just be a *disaster*. Bobby has two of the most spoiled French poodles, and they'd make Mr. Jingles's life a *misery*."

It seemed to me that Mr. Jingles could have been confined to a room or two but maybe, I thought, Bobby hadn't asked her or didn't want her and she was saving herself the embarrassment of having to admit it. I asked Jerry if he could find something for her to do in his store. "I worry what's going to happen to her. She seems so unrealistic about her future. I don't think she understands how serious her situation is. I think she could become homeless."

Delilah didn't know anything about men's clothing, nor did she know about men. And Jerry didn't need another salesperson. But he hired Delilah to do part-time secretarial work and run errands. She turned out to be an exemplary employee. Although she was very slow and deliberate, she was pathologically neat. She cleaned up the filing system, arranged his desk drawers so he could actually find things, and presented him with a telephone book redone in her small, tight script. She even placed carefully folded white linen guest towels and fragrant bars of rose-scented soap from I. Magnin in the employee bathroom—although everyone was afraid of wrinkling the towels and still used the paper towel dispenser. She didn't exactly turn it into the bathroom at I. Magnin, but it was a lot nicer than before.

She was now living in the next town, in a rooming house. Her fellow tenants were mostly foreign workers who shared the refrigerator in the communal kitchen. Someone was always taking her cottage cheese, though it was clearly labeled. She became friends with a student from China—a young woman who was getting her Ph.D. in physics up at the university. It gave us a sense of relief knowing Delilah had someone besides us. Mr. Jingles lived in Jerry's office at work and had the cleanest litter box of any cat in the history of the world.

Delilah didn't complain about her life. Her emotions were so tamped down, I doubt she even felt them. I come from a family of chronic complainers, so for me her lack of hysteria and hand-wringing were an unaccustomed pleasure.

When Thanksgiving came, I asked Delilah if she had any plans.

"Oh, I probably won't be doing too much. I suspect I'll be tired from spending the day outdoors birdwatching."

I couldn't imagine how sad it would be spending Thanksgiving in a rooming house. I asked if she'd like to join us.

"That would be looove-ly," she said in her calm, complaisant way.

We have a rather boisterous Jewish family and Delilah was neither. Her odd manner and conversational flatness could be a little unnerving, and her lack of cultural references made her seem as if she'd just arrived from Kansas. Our children thought she was weird. But I sat her between my mother, who disapproves of most people anyway, and our friend Nancy Berry, who's very outgoing and already knew Delilah from shopping at Magnin's.

Usually I can't recall jokes, but that evening Jerry told one I remember because I worried it was a little too risqué—not for my eighty-nine-year-old mother, but for Delilah. It was about a man who went to a psychiatrist because he couldn't stop thinking of women's breasts. As the doctor starts doing word association—cantaloupes ("big luscious breasts"), lemons ("small perky breasts")—everything reminds the patient of breasts. Finally the doctor says, "Windshield wipers." And the man says, "Breasts." The doctor is astounded. "How do you get 'breasts' from 'windshield wipers'?" Then Jerry imitated the wipers by turning his head left then right then left then right, and made kissing sounds as if he were kissing two breasts. I looked at Delilah to see her reaction. Delilah was *laughing*. Followed by an "Oh, *dear*." It wasn't exactly a knee-slapping belly laugh, but it was as animated as I'd ever seen her. Delilah seemed to thoroughly enjoy herself that evening and as Jerry told joke after joke, she kept saying after each punch line, "Oh, my *goodness*." "Oh, *dear*."

That night when all the guests were gone and Jerry and I were in the kitchen cleaning up, we congratulated ourselves on doing such a good deed.

"I think we've probably saved Delilah's life," he said.

At work, the salesmen started joking with Delilah, gently ribbing her, trying to tickle her extremely recessive funny bone. Even Jerry got silly with her, because it was the only way to get a reaction. He started calling her—The Deli.

"If anyone wants lunch," he'd say to his salesmen, "just get something from The Deli."

"Oh, *dear*," she'd say, "oh, *dear*."

Someone broke into Delilah's room at the rooming house. It wasn't enough her cottage cheese was always getting stolen; now her good watch with the tiny round face and black leather strap was gone. Poor Delilah. She was so disturbed by the event we told her she could stay in our playhouse with Mr. Jingles until she found another place to live. The playhouse had been built as an orchid shed by the previous owners, and we'd had it insulated and soundproofed so our son could play his drums—although the soundproofing never entirely worked, as the neighbors soon informed us. It had neither a kitchen nor a full bathroom, but it did have a sink and toilet. Now that our son was no longer interested in the drums—thank god—Jerry and I used it as a workout room. It wasn't exactly the ideal situation for Delilah, but what choice was there? We moved the treadmill, bench, and weights into the garage and Jerry got her a small refrigerator. She arrived one Saturday with a mover in a pickup truck who carried in her single bed, microwave, hot plate, and electric kettle. Delilah used the shower off the laundry room—tiptoeing in the back door and keeping it so clean it looked better than when no one was using it.

Having Delilah around was like living with Miss Marple and Martha Stewart. I'd open the linen closet and smell little bouquets of rosemary and lavender she'd placed on the towels and sheets. Our refrigerator shelves were arranged like a still life. The Sunbrella cushions on our patio furniture were stain-free, and the glass-topped table was Windexed every single day. Often I'd find her on the patio right outside our bedroom, deadheading the lavender or sweeping the fallen oak leaves. I suppose it was her way of thanking us. But besides cleaning, ironing her blouses and handkerchiefs, polishing her Bruno Magli shoes, and setting her hair, I couldn't figure out what Delilah did with her evenings. Her meager possessions were in storage. There was no TV or radio in the playhouse. There were no books, except for her bird books. She didn't care about food—she had a small pot of Prince of Wales Tea every afternoon, allowed herself one modest glass of bourbon on crushed, not cubed ice, and all she seemed to eat was cottage cheese with nuts and the fruit right off our trees.

Sometimes she'd have a "date" with Bobby Bingham, who'd arrive in a 1964 baby blue Mercedes convertible and sweep her off to the Seven Oaks Golf Club for dinner. On those occasions she'd get all dressed up in one of her ancient I. Magnin frocks— a tasteful long-sleeved dress with a scarf around her neck pinned with a brooch.

After Delilah had been living in our playhouse for a couple of months, she took her clay pots out of storage and planted them with marigolds, which she placed by her door. Jerry and I realized she'd stopped looking for a place to live. She felt completely at home.

"In the meantime," Jerry said, "she's not costing us anything, except a little water, gas, and electricity. She takes good care of the house when we're gone, and we're doing a good deed."

But as the year drew to a close, I began to worry. It was one thing giving Delilah a helping hand, but Delilah was now completely dependent on our charity. We were already taking care of my mother—paying for a driver and keeping track of her bills and medical insurance. Our son was about to attend Bard, which wasn't cheap. We were subsidizing our daughter's apartment in L.A. and paying tuition at a Catholic high school for the child of our gardener. As far as I knew, Delilah had no family or friends except for Bobby Bingham. Plus, she was getting to an age, like an old car, where things start to go wrong. I worried that Delilah was positioning us to take care of her.

When we heard Saks Fifth Avenue was opening where I. Magnin had been, Jerry and I rejoiced. Although it would cut into Jerry's business, at least Delilah could get a real job, move into a place of her own, and get more complete health insurance. Jerry suggested to Delilah she apply early before all the jobs were taken.

"I don't think I could ever be in a corporate environment again," she said quite simply.

"I think we have to stop being so subtle," I said to Jerry, "or she's never going to leave. And I'm ready to have my house back. I can't even walk around the bedroom in my underwear or relax on the patio without Delilah appearing. She has no life except the life she gets from us. I don't think she even *wants* her own life. She's like a grown-up Goldilocks."

"She reminds me of those old women in Brooklyn," Jerry said, "who'd sit at their apartment window with their elbows on the ledge, watching everything that goes on in the street below."

Jerry was right. In her own delicate, birdlike way, Delilah gathered snippets of information and seemed to know our neighbors' business. The Toppings were having marital difficulties. The Kornblatts were trying "desperately" to get into Rancho Esperanza Country Club, which had rejected them. The young widow next door had moved to Rancho Esperanza in order to meet a rich man.

It made us wonder what kind of information she was gathering about us. We whispered to each other in bed, calling her Goldilocks because we were afraid she'd hear us with the windows open, trying to figure out the best way to ask her to leave. Goldilocks became our main topic of conversation.

Jerry thought he could handle it better than I could. "Everything shows on your face," he told me. "Let me take care of it. I'll tell her when the time is right."

But Jerry never could find the right time. First Delilah found a lump in her breast. While she was waiting for the news—it turned out to be benign—we couldn't say anything. Then Bobby Bingham died, and of course *that* wasn't the right time to tell her we no longer wanted her living with us. Then Thanksgiving rolled around again, then Christmas, then the slow season in the store when we went to Italy and Delilah took care of Sparky. In the spring, I finally told Jerry he had to do it.

"Tell her we need the place for Ian's film projects. Tell her we're turning it into your home office." But Delilah's birthday was coming up and Jerry wanted to wait. He didn't want to ruin her day. She was looking forward to driving the Chinese student to the Nipomo dunes to show her the snowy plover in its nesting habitat. The day before Delilah was set to leave, our gardener noticed a couple tires on her Karmann Ghia had tire wall abrasions, which could cause a blowout on the freeway.

"The snowy plover will be the death of her yet," Jerry said. For her birthday, he had four new tires put on her car.

"Jerry, I'm overwhelmed," Delilah said, as if she'd just taken a double dose of Thorazine.

"I think she realizes we've done everything we can for her," Jerry said. "I think she'll feel indebted to us now. I don't think we'll have a problem."

But even after we told her we were redoing our living arrange-
ments, she made no effort to move. Jerry and I circled apartments
in the paper and left them on the chair by her marigold pots. Until
she could get that job at Saks, we offered to pay the security deposit on her apartment, but she found something wrong with every
place she saw.

When my mother fell and broke her hip, Jerry and I drove to
L.A. and called Delilah from the hospital telling her we had to
spend the night.

"Don't worry about a thing," Delilah said. "Sparky and I will
be just fine."

"You see?" Jerry said. "You were so anxious to get rid of her.
What would we do if we didn't have her?"

When we finally got home a couple days later, I avoided Delilah
and went straight to my bedroom. All I wanted was to crawl between clean sheets and forget about catheters and nursing homes
and a mother who would now need a live-in nurse to take care
of her. I swallowed an Ambien and pulled back the covers of
our bed. There, on the white pillowcase fragrant with an old-
fashioned rose perfume, was a strand of wavy red hair.

The next day, we found a studio apartment, used ourselves as
a reference, and put down the deposit. When we came home, we
found Delilah in her straw hat and gardening gloves, repotting
her marigolds.

"I'll handle it," Jerry told me before I could say anything. Then
he asked Delilah if she would join us at the patio table for a glass
of iced tea.

"How lovely," she said.

When we were all seated, Jerry began the delicate negotiation
to extricate ourselves.

"Renee and I have talked to you about our need to turn the
playhouse into a space where Ian can do his film projects," he

began. "Of course, your living here was always supposed to be a temporary situation, and I'm sure it hasn't been easy for you being without a kitchen and full bathroom. But we've found you a place, just a few miles away, and I think you'll really like it."

"I'm not leaving here," she said, her eyes growing wide with fear. "You're going to have to throw me out in the street."

"But Delilah," Jerry said as if he were talking to a child, "you can't stay here forever."

"*You owe me!*" she said in a voice trembling with rage. "*You owe me!*"

Delilah stated in her deposition that both Jerry and our son smoked pot, and that she had personally seen Jerry "walking around the garden like a zombie." Since she was the only female employee in a men's store, she had endured a "good-old-boy atmosphere" where all the males told off-color jokes that humiliated her. She swore she was subjected to jokes about women's breasts *even on Thanksgiving.*" Furthermore, she lived at our house without kitchen or bathroom facilities, and was a "virtual maid" who cleaned the house, did the gardening, and took care of the dog. All of which she did without compensation. Her lawyer concluded that Delilah was subjected not only to a hostile work environment, but sexual harassment. Our lawyer told us it would cost more money to fight her in court than to settle.

"I can't settle," Jerry said. "My moral outrage won't let me."

"Just remember," the lawyer said, "this isn't about justice. She's a poor working woman and you took advantage of her helplessness. Juries hate rich people. You are rich. Therefore, you are hateful."

Jerry couldn't sleep. I couldn't sleep. We argued constantly about whose fault it was. I tried to meditate and ended up on antidepressants. Jerry began medication for anxiety. Every time we had to pay a legal bill I thought Jerry was, quite literally, going to have a heart attack. One day we were hiking and Jerry experienced shortness of breath and tightness in his chest. I drove him to the hospital, where he had emergency cardiac angioplasty. The next day we told our lawyer we'd settle with Delilah Porter.

Delilah now works in Saks Fifth Avenue. It's the only department store in town, but I never use the front entrance because it's right by women's shoes. I sneak in the back, by scarves and belts. If I ever see Delilah Porter again I don't know what I'll do. I even went to a therapist because I couldn't stop thinking about it. She told me Delilah is a damaged person who has a destructive pattern of punishing anyone who gets too close. That she acts from some deep, emotional malfunction stemming from her abusive father. So I try to be Buddhist about the whole thing because I believe that good thoughts affect your life, and forgiveness and compassion bring peace. But then someone will repeat something she has said about us, and I realize she's the most dangerous person I know. I think what makes me hate her most is what she told my friend Nancy Berry. According to Nancy, Delilah said that just because I shopped at I. Magnin, it still didn't make me a lady.

The M&R Beach Chair Operating Company
Ian Green

The Englander School was founded over seventy-five years ago and is considered one of the West Coast's elite prep schools. At least according to the brochure, which shows students with open books in their laps sitting under the *two-hundred-year-old majestic oak trees*. I attended the Englander School from seventh grade through twelfth and I never once saw anyone sitting there. As a matter of fact, they specifically tell you *not* to. The majestic oaks are always losing limbs and if a majestic limb ever dropped on someone's head, their parents would find a really expensive lawyer and sue the majestic shit out of the Englander School. All the picnic tables are under the sycamore trees and if you want to study outside, *that's* where you're supposed to sit.

My first year there, the school had *A Masked Ball in Venice* as the theme for their annual fund-raiser. My mom was on the decorations committee chaired by Freyda Ball. My dad knows Freyda "from the Beverly Hills days," and calls her "a pushy broad." For the silent auction, all the mothers get people to donate things. There's also a live auction where they put the really big

donations—like this Mexican restaurant will come to your house
with a mariachi band and do a dinner for ten. Or you can be an
"extra" in a movie. The one that brought in the most money that
year was a trip to Italy donated by none other than Freyda and
Fred Ball. The lucky bidder got to fly there on "the Freds'" jet
and stay with them for a whole week in Umbria. Woo hoo! It went
for something like thirty thousand dollars.

Our family doesn't have a private plane and my dad's not a
movie producer, so for the silent auction he donated merchandise from his men's clothing store. Thousands of dollars' worth
of cashmere sweaters because my mom felt pressured to give as
much as everyone else. I know this because my mom can't stand
Freyda Ball and is constantly talking about her. One time my mom
changed her hairstyle and Freyda said to her, "Oh. You got your
hair cut." My mom got all bent out of shape about this because
Freyda never complimented her on how it looked. Another time
my mom was carrying a rug sample and bumped into Freyda.
According to my mom, Freyda said, "That's a sad little carpet.
Maybe for the maid's room."

My mom doesn't like Fred Ball either. She's always telling
the story about the time our next-door neighbor, Sally Topping,
invited Englander School parents to her house for an "Englander
School Parents Get Together." Sally is a *really* enthusiastic person who has *really* enthusiastic twin girls who also went to Englander. Every time I see Sally she wants to high-five me. I have
no idea why. She'll say something like, "I hear you just got back
from New York. All riiiiight!" and then you have to smack palms
with her. She has "make your own pizza" parties and in the seventh grade she organized an event where you "volunteer" to pick
up all the trash slobby people toss out of their cars. Everyone was
assigned certain streets and given plastic gloves, an orange plas-

tic bag like you see convicts using on the sides of freeways, and an orange T-shirt that said FIRST ANNUAL ENGLANDER SCHOOL CLEAN UP DAY (*SPONSORED BY RANCHO ESPERANZA SAVINGS AND LOAN*). You wouldn't believe some of the stuff we found, including photos some dork took of his own penis. By the time I graduated I had six orange T-shirts, which my mom gave to the maid for her relatives in Mexico. Sally's very corny and old-fashioned but the point is she's also a really nice person who never says anything bad about anyone. My mom and dad thought her Englander School Parents Get Together party was very "neighborly," but the next day they were out to dinner and the Freds came over to their table. Fred Ball said to my parents, "What did you think of the food last night? Did you ever taste anything *worse* in your *life*?" My mom does a really good imitation of Freyda saying, "I haven't seen deviled eggs and clam dip since Ike and Mamie and *The Kraft Hour*." Whenever my mom goes on a jag about Freyda Ball, my dad does a whole routine where he tries to calm her down. "Renee. Renee. Being critical is her power. Just don't engage her. Don't forget, I knew her from the Beverly Hills days *before* she was rich. When she was still working as a personal manager to these pain-in-the-ass actors. She'd bring them into the store to buy clothes for their auditions, and then she'd want to return things *after* they'd been *worn*. You throw a rock down there, you'll hit a dozen Freyda Balls, trust me. Do you think anyone in town would even want to *be* with the Freds if they didn't give money to things? And you think the Freds would *ever* pay for their gardener's kid's education? Of course not. Because if there's no plaque honoring them, they're not interested. The Freds are just rich, boring white people." And my mom says back to him, "Oh. You got your hair cut." My mom hated being on the decorations committee so much that afterward she talked about sending me to public school just so she'd never have to deal with Freyda Ball and the other mothers again.

If my mom hated being on the decorations committee, it was nothing compared to what she felt about the actual party. She wore a long dress she'd bought for my cousin Joel's wedding and a white mask she found in a toy store that had a fluffy white feather sticking up and rhinestones around the eyeholes. My dad wore a plain black mask, a black Hugo Boss suit, and a black cape he borrowed from my mom. He looked really stupid—like an old, bald Zorro. My mom thought it was funny to call him Antonio Banderasberg and kept asking him to put a big "Z" on Freyda Ball's forehead.

Freyda Ball and Lailani Rizzo took all the other mothers to L.A. to a costume rental place in Hollywood where they got clothes for themselves and their husbands. Lailani used to be Miss Philippines and she's really, *really* good-looking. Freyda has a real thin face and reminds me of one of those cartoon characters whose head gets caught in a rolling machine. So her face is a pancake but everything else gets squeezed down into these big rhinoceros haunches. Whenever she talks all I see are capped teeth jammed into her mouth and black lines where they meet her gums. My mom is always saying, "If she spent less on her diamonds and more on her teeth . . ." Yada yada yada. Everyone says she bought her daughter's way into the Englander School and I totally believe it because as soon as Portia Ball got accepted, her parents gave a lot of money to build the Ball Theater. You can see people are kind of afraid of Freyda so they treat her as if she's special. And she acts as if she's special. Even Lailani is really nice to her and I know for a fact Lailani thinks she's a bitch.

Steve Farkey's "All About Town" column in the *Rancho Gazette* ran a photo of Lailani and Freya with the headline WHO WERE THOSE LADIES? It should have been BEAUTY AND THE BEAST.

Freyda was wearing a blue gown with gigantic sleeves and a big white wig that poofed up about two feet. She had this mask made from peacock feathers. It didn't have an elastic band like a cheap mask, it had a fancy handle, and she was holding it up with a look on her face like, "Kiss my ass." My dad said she looked like a menopausal Marie Antoinette. After the party my mom found out that Freyda had made some put-down comment about her costume, saying, "*That* took a lot of imagination," and my mom got all depressed and said she's sorry we ever came to Rancho Esperanza and she wanted to move back to Pacific Palisades. It took my dad about a week to calm her down. She said she'd never go to an Englander School fund-raiser again. And they never did. My parents still donated the merchandise but every year they told people they'd be out of town.

If my parents didn't like the other parents and thought they were a bunch of rich, boring white people, then why did they think I'd like their kids, who were a bunch of rich, boring white kids? Just because we were the same age didn't mean we had anything in common. Before I left for college, I used to have lots of fights with my mom about this. She was always on my case because she thought I spent too much time in my room in front of the computer. She wanted me to be "more interactive with your fellow students." I kept reminding her that my fellow students were people like Portia Ball who drove a brand new BMW, and if she wanted me to have friends at Englander, then she should've bought me a new BMW, too, instead of giving me her Volvo with 150,000 miles on it.

Zane Rizzo was rich and drove a Range Rover, but he was the only other person at Englander who felt the same way I did, which was why we were friends. The fact that Zane could always get really good pot didn't hurt either. From the time we were about fifteen, Zane and I talked about getting out of Rancho Esperanza and going to film school together. We knew that one day we were going to make a small, independent film and get discovered at the Sundance Film Festival. That was where it was all going to happen. Steven Spielberg, watch out. Move over, Quentin Tarantino. Okay, maybe we weren't going to quite be Spielberg or Tarantino, but Ian Green and Zane Rizzo were definitely on their way to becoming the next Coen brothers.

Zane's father, Vince Rizzo, produces action movies. The kind of summer movie that opens big and is always number-one at the box office the first weekend. But Zane is pretty cool about the whole thing. I used to go to quite a few Hollywood movie premieres with him where the limo pulls up, you get out of the car to a bunch of screaming fans on bleachers behind these big velvet ropes, and you have to walk down the red carpet all the way into the theater. Most of the fans were weird—sort of ugly, fat girls and geeky guys. The kind of people you see on *Good Morning America* who stand behind barricades on the street holding signs saying HAPPY BIRTHDAY MOM! and wave at the camera when the weather guy tells you it's minus fifteen in North Dakota. People you'd want nothing to do with in your real life. The photographers were kind of a freak show too—mostly fat, slobby guys jostling each other and yelling, "Look over here! Over here!" And the flashbulbs were going off every half-second, blinding you if you actually *did* look over. For some reason I found it nerve-racking. Not that anyone cared who *I* was. Maybe that was the problem. It made you feel kind of stupid for being nobody. One time I did turn around and a photographer yelled, "Not *you*! *Him*!" *Him* being Bruce Willis. That *really* made me feel stupid.

The party after the movie was always a trip. One time it was in a huge airplane hangar at Santa Monica airport. It was decorated like an intergalactic-themed bar mitzvah, with all these spinning planets and asteroids zipping across the sky. Everything was very dark except for outer space, which glowed like neon because it was illuminated with black light. But if you had any fake teeth, they would glow, too, which Zane and I thought was pretty cool. I got to meet a lot of movie stars at these events. I suppose Tom Cruise was the biggest. He didn't seem that crazy to me. He was actually a very nice and normal-looking person. Except for his neon teeth.

Zane's family and my family don't socialize. Zane's step-mother, Lailani, is much younger than my mom. Zane's father is my dad's age but he's an Italian type like you'd see on *The Sopranos*. He's much better looking though than any of those guys and he wears jeans and those really soft, expensive leather jackets. But he talks like they do. You can hear him on the phone. "Fuck that guy. What a fucking asshole. Don't try to fuck with me." Even when he's just outside and it's a nice day he'll say, "What a fucking day. Is this a great fucking day or what?"

My dad says "fuck" too but not every other word. He seems much older than Vince Rizzo, probably because he's the son of Holocaust survivors and it's affected his whole life. A day doesn't go by where he doesn't refer to it in some way or another. His idea of a great vacation is to take my mom, my sister, and me to concentration camps. The Rizzos have houses in Hawaii and Deer Valley, which they donate to the Englander School fund-raiser auction, but our family goes on the grand tour of Auschwitz for our Christmas holiday. Woo hoo! Even when he's just in L.A. or Las Vegas for business, my dad always seems to run into other people who are children of Holocaust survivors. My mom says it's like they all have an identification chip planted under their skin like our dog, Sparky, and they find each other no matter where they are.

Zane's father tells stories about Hollywood and about being on location and who was fucking who. My dad tells stories about growing up in Brooklyn and how hard my grandfather had to work and how anti-Semitic the Ukrainians and the Poles are. I've heard these stories so many times even *I* know them by heart. My dad's always saying "I'm telling you these stories so you can appreciate where you've come from and that not everybody is rich and lives in Rancho Esperanza." As if I didn't already know that.

In our junior year at Englander, Mr. Samuels, our drama teacher, came up with the brilliant idea of having everyone in his class make a film. He came up with the idea probably because Zane's father donated ten HD video cameras to the school. Mr. Samuels, who'd once been a screenwriter, was going to help everyone with the scripts. You were supposed to work with a partner, so Zane and I naturally decided to team up. Because Sundance was waiting for us. The only small problem was we couldn't figure out what we wanted our movie to be about. We finally came up with snowboarding.

My dad offered to drive Zane and me up to Mammoth to go location scouting and pick up some action shots. My dad never learned to ski or do anything athletic because when he was a kid they had no money, so he had to work from the time he was about twelve. That's what started him telling us the story. Instead of just telling us, "I don't ski," he went into a whole story about what *he* was doing at sixteen. He wasn't running around making movies, that's for sure. That was the implication. The story he told was about the time he worked at the M&R Beach Chair Operating Company. M&R stands for Mendelson and Roth, who rented beach chairs and umbrellas at Coney Island near where my dad grew up. "But by the time I got there," my dad said, "Roth had already been dead a long time and it was just Mendelson. You want to know from tough Jews? Mendelson was one tough Jew who knew all the angles."

It was a long ride up to Mammoth, about five hours, and my dad has this thing where you can't listen to your iPod if you're with other people because he thinks it's rude. You have to make conversation. But with my dad it's not conversation. It's listening to him tell stories about growing up in Brooklyn. Everything with my dad is pretty negative. As if he's expecting the Holocaust to happen all over again. That's the way he was brought up. That's the way his parents must have treated him. But their world isn't the same as my world, which I keep telling my dad. I don't know any Ukrainians or Poles or Germans. Or even anyone like Mendelson. So I don't know why he keeps telling me these kinds of stories.

Zane was sitting in the backseat and when I turned around, I saw he had the tape recorder out, a really small Sony his father had given him that uses microcassettes, so it's pretty nonintrusive. We thought we'd use it in Mammoth to interview people. Zane's father said it would be helpful for dialogue when we wrote our screenplay. I didn't think Zane would be interested in my dad's stories since they never seem to have any relevance. But Zane had turned it on and was recording my dad.

"At the time I worked there Mendelson must have been only about fifty years old, but I regarded him as an old man. He *looked* like an old man, perched on a wooden stool, his cuffed brown pants fastened underneath his big stomach, and a short-sleeve shirt that barely closed. He never used his fingers to smoke his cigarette, but kept it tightly clamped between his discolored teeth," and here my dad imitated Mendelson inhaling and exhaling through a tiny opening in his mouth like Mendelson used to do. "*Sssssssss sssssssss.* Even when he coughed and choked, his lungs sounding like swamps of phlegm, the cigarette stayed put." This was also the story he told my sister and me about why we should never smoke. Because our lungs would turn into "swamps of phlegm."

"So what was Coney Island like?" Zane asked, and my dad went on. I'd heard it before, like I said, so I sort of tuned out. At the time, I didn't realize how much that story would change my entire outlook on life.

When we got up to Mammoth, we checked into the motel and then Zane and I got a half-day lift ticket and took the tape recorder with us. On the chairlift, we listened to my father's tape. The quality of the sound was surprisingly good. Then Zane turned the cassette over and we talked into the recorder about ideas we had for our screenplay about snowboarders. At the end of the weekend, we'd taken some footage of Mammoth and some pretty hot snowboarders, but we realized we didn't know what the fuck the story was about. It was only supposed to be a ten-minute film, so it's not as if you even had time to develop the characters.

When we got home we met with Mr. Samuels and told him we were having trouble with our script. First we played some of our ideas, but he thought it didn't have a story arc. Then Mr. Samuels heard some of my dad's story and he said, "Now that would be a good movie. If you were able to interview him on camera and then go back to Coney Island and film some of the places he's talking about." As soon as he said it, I got so amped. "I have cousins who live in Brooklyn," I said, "so we can stay with them and interview my aunt and ask her what she remembered about Mendelson and Coney Island and the way my dad was at sixteen." My cousins live in a neighborhood that has a hundred different places to go to within walking distance. If you feel like watching people get tattooed you can walk over to this block and then you can walk to the movies, and afterward go out for Vietnamese food, or just get some kabobs right off a street cart. On any street you can pass people who are more interesting than anyone you'll ever see in Rancho Esperanza. I figured if Zane stayed in Brooklyn with me, he could get a feeling for the place and it would definitely help the movie.

My dad was pretty excited about us focusing on his life. I positioned him in a chair in the living room, I took the phone off the hook, I put Sparky in the car where she loves to sit, and then I videotaped my dad as he told the story, once again, of the M&R Beach Chair Operating Company.

"Every morning at eight-thirty, I'd wait with the other boys in the shadow of the Tornado roller coaster. When the sun started peeking through the gray and Mendelson determined he would open up for the day, he'd yell, 'It's time to go to *work*!' and he'd unlock the tall, corrugated double doors that led to his lair underneath the boardwalk. We'd get in our group—new guys in front, experienced boys to the right. It reminded me of that scene in *On the Waterfront*. That's before your time but it was a good movie. We should rent it. Anyway, in the movie there are throngs of workers milling around waiting to be picked for that day. *Wanting* to be picked. More workers than they have jobs for. Mendelson sat on his stool and as we waited in our groups, he would choose the boys and assign us our bays. 'Shapiro, Green, and Baratto, Bay One. *Sssssssss*. McDonald, Esposito, and Bernstein, Bay Two. *Sssssssss*.' If you laughed when he coughed, and it was hard *not* to, because if one person started laughing—you know how it is when you're a kid. But if Mendelson caught you laughing, you were sent to Bay Seven. Bay One or Two in Brighton Beach was where you wanted to be. Bay One was nice, polite immigrant families, mostly Jewish. Bay Two was single people on a date trying to make a good impression, like the Yuppies today. Bays One and Two were the premier bays. They gave you a nice tip when you brought them their chairs and set up the umbrella in the sand so it wouldn't blow away. But Bay Seven was Siberia. Out by the aquarium, too far from the subway stop. It didn't attract the beach crowds. You could work all day at Bay Seven and come back with bubkes. And if you didn't produce tips, Mendelson fired you.

"Mendelson had it all worked out. Seventy-five cents an hour against your tips, which were put in a communal pot in each of the bays. If you made *more* than seventy-five cents an hour, and everyone *did* unless you were sent to Siberia, then Mendelson owed you nothing. If you *didn't* make at least seventy-five cents an hour in tips, then Mendelson fired you. The day began when the sun came out, so sometimes we stood around until noon— and of course Mendelson didn't pay you for standing around— and then you had to hustle hard until five or six at night. I learned to carry four chairs—two under each arm—*and* an umbrella. I learned to run on the hot sand with my load and set the umbrella at just the right angle. The first day I came home with shaky arms and a sunburned back and when I tried to find sympathy my father said to me, 'You never would have made it in the camps.' After that there were no complaints, only learning to make the maximum amount of tips. Even in Bay Seven, I once pulled in twenty-two dollars. An un*heard* of sum in Siberia. That's why all the boys liked working with me. Italian, Irish, it didn't matter. We came from three different high schools, but I never experienced anti-Semitism there. No one ever called me names. Because I produced. More than they did. And they respected that.

"I learned how to patrol the beach at the end of the day, and spot the ones who were too lazy or too tired to return their chairs and umbrellas. I would do it for them so they could just get back on the subway and not have to shlep. Then I got to keep the full deposit. But if a sudden rain came, there was a different method we employed. When they'd all line up to return the chairs, I'd work it out with the girl in the cage to slow it down. She'd take her time examining each deposit slip and returning the fifty cents per chair they'd laid out. When I could see the line was becoming impatient, I'd start at the back with a pocket full of quarters and I'd say, *If you don't want to wait in line, I'll give you a quarter for your chit.*

"Unless they were really cheap or really poor, they'd let me return the chair for them and keep the extra twenty-five cents, just so they could get home. It was a shameful but time-honored hustle all the experienced boys knew, and passed down to the new ones.

"Bay Seven wasn't so easy but Bay Sixteen by Stauch Bathhouse, just down from the Cyclone and the original Nathan's, was the *real* Coney Island. In Bay Seven, I worried I wouldn't make the money. In Bay Sixteen, I worried I wouldn't make it home alive. That was where the Italians and blacks went. Fights would erupt like whirling sand tornadoes that sprang up from nowhere and disappeared just as quickly. People would be standing on line for hot dogs and two seconds later, knives! Blood! Someone stepped on someone's foot. A black boy looked at a white girl the wrong way. Who the hell *knows* what set them off? And then, before the cops could even be called, the Italians would run away, and the blacks would be covered with bloody towels. Right in front of Stauch Baths I saw four Italians break Ballantine beer bottles over a black boy's head. The glass went flying in a million pieces like in the movies. They loved breaking Ballantine bottles because they were thin and broke easily. Thank god it wasn't Coke bottles. The black girlfriend was pushed down and kicked. It was one of those things where you can't even do anything to help. That time the police came right away. They lined up on horses, flank to flank, from the bay to the boardwalk, and they cleared the beach in about ten minutes. 'Pack up and go home!' they yelled into their bullhorns. 'Get the hell outta here!' Chairs and umbrellas were left in the sand, and I'd spent until sunset returning them to the cage. *That* had been a profitable day.

"I knew why the police came so quickly because I'd seen how it worked my first week on the job. I'd been sent to Bay Three with my cousin Ritchie and the girl who worked the cage, Denise. The chairs and umbrellas were kept under the boardwalk in an enclosed space, padlocked at the end of every day. Denise had the keys, but that morning a drunk was sleeping in front of the doors, curled up on newspapers, his toes poking out of filthy socks, and she refused to step over him. She said to me, 'Mendelson says we have to call the cops when there's a drunk. It's a rule.'

"So I was elected to go make the phone call, and when I returned to Bay Three, I saw a policeman with fat, pink cheeks take his nightstick and whack the sleeping drunk on the bottom of his feet. The drunk screamed in pain but he was hit again. He tried to crawl away, covering his face with his filthy hands and the cop *still* went after him, getting him on the arm and back and head. I'll never forget it, the look on the cop's face. Something between pleasure and smugness and hate. It was worse than the senseless brutality of the Italians toward the blacks because it was sanctioned. It brought back the hundreds of stories my father told of dealing with the Ukrainians or Germans or Poles. But the curious thing was, later that day I saw Mendelson hand a white envelope to two sergeants or whatever rank they were. All I remember is that they had stripes on their sleeves.

"I came home to my father, and told him all about it. He didn't say anything, just shook his head. Then I asked him, 'What do you think Mendelson was doing with the envelope?'

"'What was he *doing*?' Benny said, like he was talking to the village idiot. 'He was *paying* them.'

"'But why would he pay a policeman?' I asked.

"And my father said, 'What. You think they come so quick because they love Mendelson? Don't be so naive. If *I* call the police and if *Mendelson* calls the police, where're they going to show up first? It's *understood*.'"

That was, more or less, the end of my father's story. Zane and I decided to go to Coney Island over winter break to get the shots we needed to complete the film. A couple of days before we were set to go, my dad had to go into the hospital for emergency heart surgery, and my mom asked me to postpone the trip. Zane said we couldn't reschedule because we'd never get the footage we needed in time to make the movie. So he went without me. He ended up staying at his father's apartment in the city with one of his father's assistants. I was really disappointed I didn't get to go. Especially since it was my dad's life.

When Zane got home he showed Mr. Samuels and me the footage he took. It was some of the places my dad talked about, except it was cold and there were no people on the beach. It looked very bleak, not at all like the way my dad had described it. It wasn't the movie I'd imagined. I suggested to Mr. Samuels that we fill in with period photos of Coney Island from the 1960s and my dad and his family. That way, when my dad is talking about the beach being dotted with beach umbrellas, you can see what it actually looked like. I also suggested laying a track of old music from 1963 that would have been playing at the time.

Zane turned the footage over to me and it took me five weeks working every spare minute to edit the movie, put in the music, and get the archival photos as well as personal family photos. There were over four hundred edits. For a ten-minute film that's a lot. When I showed the completed movie to my dad he couldn't believe how professional it looked.

Zane's father invited my parents and Mr. Samuels over to their house for a screening of our movie. The Rizzos live in the biggest estate in Rancho Esperanza and have a screening room that's better than any movie theater I've ever seen. It's in an old barn and the whole downstairs has been converted into really nice offices for all the assistants and secretaries who work for them. It's decorated with these old western saddles and Navajo rugs, and on the walls are all the posters from the movies Vince Rizzo has produced. My parents have one small Navajo rug they bought on their honeymoon that no one—except maybe an old Indian—

has ever stepped on. They keep it on the back of the sofa in the living room so our dog doesn't ruin it. Zane's parents have so many of them that some are just folded up in stacks like the towels around their pool. My mom couldn't get over how many Navajo rugs they had. The actual screening room is upstairs, which was where the guy who took care of the horses used to live. Everything's been kept very rustic and there are these awesome red leather chairs and ottomans. You lean back, put your feet up, and grab one of the fur throws they keep around just in case anyone gets cold. Now that's the way to watch a movie. There's also a professional popcorn machine and a bar with black-and-white cowhide barstools.

Mr. Samuels said it was the best student film he'd ever seen and the editing was extremely sophisticated because it kept the visuals from ever getting static. He especially liked the way I moved the camera when I did the shots of the old photos. Sometimes I'd slowly pan the photo left to right and sometimes I'd zoom in really slow. The Ken Burns Effect. He also thought the music set a tone and rhythm for the entire piece. Mr. Samuels submitted our movie for a student film award where you're in competition with students from all over the state. I couldn't believe when it actually won first prize.

But when we went to get the award, only Zane was invited. Because he had put himself down as the director and producer. He put me down as art director and editor. I'd let him do it because, basically, it was his father's camera and his father's money financing the film. The thing is, anyone could have taken the footage he took. I only used a couple of his shots anyway—some newspapers blowing on the beach, the Cyclone roller coaster, and a homeless man scrounging around in a garbage can. That was basically Zane's contribution. Zane didn't even do his own camera work because a professional his father knew was helping him with every shot. The fun part and the real work was in doing all the editing and mixing and basically putting the whole thing together on the computer.

Zane used our movie and the award to get accepted into USC film school. My dad was really angry and kept telling me to confront him—that the award should have gone to both of us and I was naive to let him take all the credit. He even spoke to Mr. Samuels, who told my dad it was out of his hands.

But I know the real reason Mr. Samuels wouldn't say anything: because the Rizzos let the Englander School hold their annual fundraiser on their estate. Because the Rizzos donate the use of their vacation houses for the auction. And because Mr. Samuels wrote a screenplay and asked Zane if he would give it to his dad to read.

I told my parents it didn't matter. I don't need the glory of the red carpet. I'm not cut out for Hollywood anyway, from what I've seen of it. I don't really need a bunch of fat, ugly girls screaming my name. Besides which, film is a collaborative medium and I just like to do my own thing. I've really gotten into documentaries. I've watched all of Michael Moore's movies at least three times, and the whole *Seven Up* series, where this English director started with kids when they were only seven, and interviews them every seven years until they're married with children of their own. It's a lot more interesting than the kind of movie Vince Rizzo produces.

I think back to that day my dad drove Zane and me up to Mammoth so we could make a movie about snowboarding. It took me a while to figure out the relevance of his story, but now I get it: Vince Rizzo is Mendelson, Mr. Samuels is the cop on the take, Zane is the type who expects someone else to return his rentals, and I'm the guy running on the hot sand with four chairs and an umbrella. The Englander School, Rancho Esperanza, and, come to think of it, maybe the whole world is just a bigger version of the M&R Beach Chair Operating Company.

"Yes" and "No." That's all the English what I speak when I come
to this country. How I get here is my older sister was living in
Los Angeles, California, at that time and I was in Honduras. My
sister she worked for a lawyer and sometime she send money to
me, but not all the time. When I pregnant with my daughter I am
sixteen and my father was very, very mad with me because I don't
marry. I was the only one who didn't go to the church with a
beautiful white dress and he don't support me. I never marry the
father because his family was terrible to me. They was too nose
up. Because he was a guy who go to the university and he have
more school than I because we were poor. His family was disappointed with me. When my daughter was born, I have to go to
live with my boyfriend's parents and they were so mean with
me always. When my daughter was a baby and cry they say to
me, "Go outside with that girl because she cry too much." Everyone knows babies cry very often but they always complain and it
make me very upset. I stay there until my daughter was one year
old then I move to my cousin and her husband. My boyfriend's

parents send him to Mexico City for school just because that's the way we no see each other. But when he come back, we fall in love and we start to date again and that's how I got pregnant with my son. All that time I never pressure him to marry me. Never ever. The father of my children, he marry and he forgot us completely and he never support us. He broke my feelings. After that, I'm scared for me to find another guy.

I move onto a small piece of land my father own, and there is a little house. But it's more a shack than a house. I do everything to make money. I made tortillas for this lady who have a restaurant because this lady made breakfast for my children. She pay me a little bit of money and give me lunch and dinner. So I say okay. I have the food and that's more important. My skin from making tortillas and cooking them on the fire all day was so red. My arms are all just red. I went to picking coffee. Forty-pound bags I put on my shoulder up and down the hill. I pressing clothes, do laundry and in Honduras do laundry is by hand. No washing machine. I was so poor with my two children and no husband and my house all coming apart and no roof and my older sister say to me on the telephone, "The only way I can help you, Fidelia, is if you move to come here to the United States."

My sister she no send me money for a ticket. She pay somebody to move me and she send me forty dollars for the food on my trip. It take me one week. Six person came in that car and we crossed all of Mexico. It's a big experience for me. I have no idea what to expect. We make many stops and we throw our clothes away because there was no way to bring anything. We drive and drive and for one day we travel in a big boat to Tijuana and we wait there for the coyote.

The first time we tried to cross the border by the mountain. There was another woman with me in the trunk of the car. But *la Migra* arrest us. I try to speak like a Mexican and I say I'm from Mexico. Because to go back all the way to Honduras is so far. In the afternoon they take us to Tijuana and they say we have to go back. But the same night we try to cross the border and we did. When I finally cross the border it was Christmas day. I get out of the trunk and it's dark and cold and I say, "If one day I go back to see my children, for sure I don't want to come in the same way."

The first stop we make after the border was in San Diego. We get there and we stay in an apartment for a couple hours and sleep. Then another person came over and move us to Los Angeles. It was on Saturday morning early, the sun come up, and we stop for a coffee. A Taco Bell! I say to myself, we are in United States! I have no idea what was the half and half for the coffee. I say, what's this? All so new! I remember everything for me was so good!

Then we go to an apartment on Western Avenue, I remember the street name, and a new person there and that person say, "You can take a shower." In Honduras we don't have hot water. So I start screaming with the steam because he forgot to explain to me which one was hot and which one was cold. That person, he do the laundry for me because I only have one clothes and we wait until my sister come. And I wait for my sister the whole day because my sister is very religious and she go to the church. She finally come for me at six o'clock at night.

I'm lucky when I got here because I start working right away in a factory in Los Angeles. But the Chinese people take advantage. Because what they do is they pay so little. Nothing. I sewing and they say you have to do the collar. They pay eight cents for one. So you have to do one hundred collars for eight dollars. I work there for six months pressing clothes and doing whatever to send money to my other sister who was taking care of my children. But I'm lucky because my sister in Los Angeles, in the church she say, "I have my sister here and she want to work in a house where she can live." And I find Señorita Hadley, who live in Hancock Park.

When they call me for the interview number one I was nervous. But Señorita Hadley speak Spanish so I say, "I don't need to talk to no one but Señorita Hadley." But I start learning English and I watch TV. *Sesame Street*. That was September. By November her mother die and she tell me she go live in Rancho Esperanza because she have to take care of the house. I have no idea where Rancho Esperanza is, but I feel okay with her so I say, "I can go wherever you go." So I move to here and I'm here now for twenty-one years.

The first week when we move to here for me it was paradise. It's a big estate called Casa de las Flores. Now I know what that means, *estate*. That's a big house. A big property. I didn't know before what that means. It's a big house and I have two rooms and my own bathroom. The only thing there was only one bus run around Rancho Esperanza every hour but it was so exciting. On Saturday, my day off, I take the Greyhound to go to my sister in Los Angeles. But the second Saturday I tell Señorita Hadley I want to stay because I want to start learning how to move in Rancho Esperanza. She was planning a trip to Europe for a month and I have to stay here alone so I need to know the city. Señorita Hadley take me to the town and say, "Okay, I leave you here. Go walk and see the name of the streets. And when you tired and ready to go home just call and let me know where you are and I come and pick you up." So that's the way I learn my way.

When she get back from Europe she start to talk to me about a lawyer to get my papers and be able to live here. And she look for classes for me to go to school and I start going to high school at night for ESL class. And then little by little I say, I don't want to go to Los Angeles every weekend. I prefer to stay here.

When I start my case with the lawyer he say, in three years you be ready, and that was not true. And there's no choice to go home when you start the case. Because if I go to Honduras I never be able to come back. Even when my little son die because he have a bad heart, I cannot go back for his funeral and that make me cry for a long time. I explain to my daughter many time there was no choice. So I stay here and I support my daughter to go to school and pay for typing class and English class. I say to her, if I stay there I don't have money to do that. So I left my children in Honduras and I no see my daughter for ten years. And I never see my son again. But every time I go back, I go to see his grave.

When Señorita Hadley died from cancer I was very sad. I think I had to look for my own place and that scared me because I never pay rent. I got everything with her. But Mr. Bobby who is Señorita Hadley's friend move into the house to take care of the two dogs Jock and Joe. And he say to me, "You can live here but I can't afford to pay you every day so you have to find other work." I met people when I work for Señorita Hadley so that was not too hard finding work. Soon I had lots of clients and I work for Mr. Bobby two afternoons a week.

Mr. Bobby, he was my friend. He talk to me. He tell me everything. You know everybody has good days or sad days and problem days and he say to me, "Something happened to you," and I say, "How you know?" and he say, "Because you always smile. What happened? What's the matter?" He always say that to me and the same for him. When I see him I say, "What's going on in your life?"

So I take care of the house and we become very good friends. And then he push me to drive. He always screaming to me, "A million people drive. What happened to you? You have to learn to drive. I teach you." Mr. Bobby he take me in the Mercedes on Sunday morning to drive and I remember my neck hurt I was so tense. All we do is driving on the same street and back on the same street always looking for the stop sign. He say, "I give you the money for a car but you have to pay me back." He say, "Look for not a fancy car because you have to get experience first." So I talk to my brother-in-law in Los Angeles who work in a dealer and he say, "There is a car for fifteen hundred dollars. It's a small car and if you want come over and see it." A Mitsubishi Galant. And I tell Mr. Bobby and he say, "Okay I give you the check." And I say, "I give you two hundred dollar a month." I start working cleaning an office around here in Rancho Esperanza and that money I pay him the second week each month. And I start making the payments and when I owe him five hundred dollars he say, "Okay, that's it. The car's yours. Completely. Forget about the other money." And I started driving everywhere.

Mr. Bobby always say, "You have to take care of me, Fidelia, when I get old," and I say, "You better let me give you a bath," and we laugh. It was so sad when he died. I said I would take care of him. He was my friend. When he died I was the only person in charge of the house because the lawyer was on a cruise. I remember the lawyer contact me and he say, "Fidelia, you in charge." Because Mr. Bobby's family never came over from New York to see what happened. When I have to pack his things in boxes it was so sad for me. He has a problem with his family. That's why he always say he run away from the family. Because they never accept that he was gay. It was so sad because he was a very good person. When I met Mr. Bobby he never told me about his life until later. But I'm not stupid. I see something is going on here. He has a girlfriend named Delilah but I know he's gay. I say to him, "How come Delilah never marry?" and he say, "She was in love with a man but he married the rich girl." And I say to him, "So maybe *you* should marry her," and he say, "I want to marry the rich girl, *too*." And we laugh.

I still work at Casa de las Flores for the new owners, Mr. and Mrs. Kornblatt. They spend two years remodeling the house with Mr. Laguna and they put in new this and new that. But they no live here all the time. Mrs. Kornblatt is very fussy. Everything has to be just so. She tell me to make endive filled with smoked salmon and little green things on top—I forget the name. And she say put them on the plate like *this*. She too fancy. She talk to me in a fancy way. She has a lot of old, expensive things and she say, "You have to be very careful with this because this dish is from *this* century or *that* century" and I have no idea. For me it's just a dish. I don't know about centuries. When she entertain they have a cook and catering and after they leave I have to count all the glasses and all the dishes to make sure they all there. They have four sets of dishes so for me it's too complicated.

She have this big round magnifying mirror in her dressing room in a silver frame. It's on her dressing table and she say to me, "Fidelia, this mirror is very expensive. Mr. Laguna get it for me so be very careful when you polish it." Then I find the bill from Mr. Laguna on her desk when I'm dusting and I see it cost seven thousand dollars. For a mirror. It's a very nice mirror but you can get one at Longs drugstore for seven dollars.

Or she want me to make toasted bread with goat cheese and olive tapenade from Trader Joe's that she ask me to buy for her and she say, "Fidelia, you forgot to toast the bread." And I say, "No, I didn't. The bread is toasted." And she look and she say, "But it's not toasted *enough*." Everything with her is always "but." "This is good *but* . . ." She like me to make them soup. Mr. Kornblatt he like black bean soup. So I make it and she say, "Fidelia, this is good *but* why you no put in the ham bone?" And I say, "Because you tell me you want Mr. Kornblatt to lose weight that's why." Mr. Kornblatt he is *gordito* and he always saying when I cook, "Fidelia, you have to help me to lose weight." But he never exercise. If he go walk he pay someone to go with him. And they go to the track and they walk in a circle. Now Mrs. Kornblatt has a personal assistant. I say, "What you need an assistant for?" And she say, "To drive me to the hairdresser." She comes from New York and she no drives on the freeway to L.A. She will only drive close. They have too many people working for them. All the time people around doing this and doing that. Last week they replace the sink in the laundry room with a big stone sink and Mr. Laguna he come to put flower vases above the sink on shelves. So now Mrs. Kornblatt can cut flowers in the stone sink. Why she can't cut flowers in the old sink like Señorita Hadley? They always saying, "Fidelia, we want you to work for us more days." And I say, "I can't. I have other people I work for." When they here they want somebody all the time working. What I say is, why people have to be dependent on other people for something that you can do yourself? I think because maybe they have too much and they say, "I can pay for anything." And Mrs. Kornblatt doesn't want anyone to speak Spanish. She want all the people who work for her to speak English. So I come in the morning and I say to Mr. Kornblatt, "Good morning" and he say, "*Buenos días.*" And I say, "Are you feeling well?" and he say, "*Más o menos.*" And I say *this* in English and he say *that* in Spanish and I turn to Mrs. Kornblatt and I say, "I try. Don't blame me."

And everywhere they have refrigerators. They have two big refrigerators in the kitchen. They have a refrigerator in the pool house. They have a refrigerator in the library so they can fix their drinks. They have a refrigerator in the upstairs sitting room so they don't have to go downstairs to get their drinks because it's too far to walk. They have a refrigerator in the exercise room and one in the media room and there's also a refrigerator in the guest-house. And all the refrigerators have to have six of everything. Six Fuji waters, six Pellegrino, six Coca-Colas, six this and six that, and I have to check every time I go there. I go to all eight refrigerators and make sure there are six of everything. And Mrs. Kornblatt say, "Fidelia, did you check the refrigerators?" and I say, "I check and everything have six." Now Mr. Laguna say to take out the refrigerator by the pool and put in another bathroom there. They are always working on their house. And Mr. Kornblatt is always complaining that Mr. Laguna is too expensive. I say to Mr. Kornblatt, "Why you have to live that way? Why you have to live with all these worries?" I always ask myself that question, why? It is better to live simple. Too much stress. All this worry for little things.

One day Mrs. Kornblatt say she having people over and I should remember the names of the rooms. It's not the living room it's the drawing room. It's not the TV room it's the media room. I tell her it's too complicated for me, all these different names. At this party she serve fruit punch with mint and she want me to serve and I should wear white gloves when I serve the fruit punch. It was for lunch. When she say that I tell Alfonso, the gardener, "She want me to wear white gloves. Where you buy white gloves? I have to call Michael Jackson." And we laugh.

But I do my job. When people say "poor Fidelia," I don't like. People say "poor Fidelia" because I'm single. I say, Poor *no*. It's *my* choice. Sometime I like to have somebody to go out with and I like to dance but I don't want to be with anybody. I'm happy single. I can do whatever I want. My daughter live here now and my granddaughter. I work with different people and I'm happy with my clients. If somebody don't respect me, I don't work for those people. I just quit. Clean house is a job. It's just a job. I don't have to feel less than the other people. Yes, they lucky to have more school and more opportunities to go to university but when I see the rich people I don't feel at all that I'm less. I am a strong person. That's how I feel.

For sure someday I want to go back to Honduras. Because in the United States if you don't prepare for your old age you cannot live here. I still have my house in Honduras and I took that piece of property and built a new house. Now I help my family when I can. They say to me, I can't believe how your life change. But if I get sick I can't work anymore. In Honduras there is more family to take care of me so I don't have to be alone. I met an old lady every time I go there. Selling avocados in one corner of the market where the sun is very hot and I stop to buy avocados from her and I say, "Where's your family?" and she say, "My children and everybody go different places." So I say, "Where you live?" And she say she rent space in a house with somebody. And I saw this old lady tired and with no shoes because she says the plastic shoes they was very old. The next time I go there I look for that lady and I give her clothes and I give her shoes and it make me feel good that I can do that. Now when I go home, people think I am the rich lady. I say to them, I'm not rich. I only have one refrigerator. But they don't understand the joke.

Scandal
Fernando Laguna

Architectural Digest put out a Special Design Issue recently in which they posed a question to me and fourteen of my fellow designers: Who and what have most influenced your personal style?

Who: *Hadley Stevens and Bobby Bingham, without a doubt. Neither were designers, but both possessed exquisite taste and a contagious passion for living.*

What: *Casa de las Flores. In spite of its modest Spanish name, it is a majestic stone Italianate villa in Rancho Esperanza. Hadley's parents built the estate early in the last century and there she had grown up riding horses, meandering through forty acres of magnificent gardens, socializing with artists and tycoons alike, and enjoying a life of privilege most of us can only imagine. "Casa" was the first truly grand estate with which I'd become acquainted. I was struck not only by the authenticity of detail and elegant proportions, but by the sense of timelessness it evoked. The massive front gate with its sixteenth-century Venetian statuary was not just an entrance of uncommon distinction, but a portal into a more beautiful age. After Hadley's untimely death, her close friend Bobby Bingham moved into her home and added his own refined sensibilities. As the years passed, the Casa took on the mien of a once beautiful diva whose good bones were still evident in spite of time's ravages. Bobby was the final occupant before it was sold to the current owners, who, fortunately, gave me the opportunity to restore Casa de las Flores to its former glory. Together, Hadley and Bobby inspired my belief that creating beautiful and elegant surroundings is not just a profession but, one can almost say, a divine calling.*

There was, of course, much more to the story, but *Architectural Digest* was hardly the place to share it.

Bobby introduced me to Rancho Esperanza in 1976. It was still just a sleepy, provincial village the first time I saw it. There were only two or three decent restaurants (the private clubs weren't much better), but what it lacked in cuisine, it more than made up for in character: the mild, Mediterranean climate, the fishermen in picturesque little boats unloading their catch by the docks, and the town itself—all whitewashed walls and terra-cotta roofs reminiscent of a hillside village in Andalusia. Rancho Esperanza always attracted its share of money and beauty; more Hollywood stars than I can name used our little paradise for their lost weekends. They typically headed straight for the pool at the Biltmore or to Scandal, a restaurant known for its thick steaks and stiff drinks. It was fun to rub elbows at dinner or see them strolling along the beaches, but come Sunday they knew enough to fly away home. A few came back to make Rancho Esperanza their permanent address but soon discovered it wasn't a town easily impressed. We had our homegrown share of serial philanderers, flamboyant alcoholics, and beautiful wastrels—we certainly didn't need anyone *new* showing us how it was done, thank you very much. Back then, as now, the Rancho Esperanza Country Club didn't accept people from the entertainment industry; they knew what they had and wanted to keep it that way. And what they had were members who understood that money should never shout. Money should whisper.

I'd drive up from L.A. on Friday after my last class and stay with Bobby, who lived in a bungalow two blocks from the beach. We'd met at Cal Arts where he'd briefly been my teacher and had taken an interest in my work. There was never anything serious between us. Bobby was years my senior and, at the time, enamored with Ramón, a young Mexican who worked as a groom on the largest estate in Rancho Esperanza. Bobby would never admit to being gay; he thought of himself as a sensual person who expressed himself in many ways. Though, as far as I know, Bobby never had sex with any of the women he dated. He nurtured a lifelong fantasy—*châteaux en Espagne*—that one day Hadley Stevens would marry him. He said that with her looks and his taste they could conquer the world.

Always a connoisseur of beauty and wealth, he possessed neither himself. What Bobby had was *élan*, one of the few things money cannot buy. "If only the people with money had taste and the people with taste had money," he always said. I thought it a shame he never capitalized on his own taste. There's no doubt he would have made the fortune he coveted and become a designer of influence. No one ever knew for certain if Bobby was brought up with money or just pretended to be. His family was from New York but he never spoke much of them, except to mention that his father always made his mother a "dressing drink," which they'd sip as they were getting ready to go out. According to Bobby, it was the only family tradition worth embracing. Whatever his finances, I believe Bobby never felt the need to work. Striving was gauche and somehow beneath him. He brings to mind a quote I'd read in school a long time ago, attributed to Julius Caesar: *I would rather be first in a little Iberian village than second in Rome.* New

York was too big for Bobby, Los Angeles too flashy, but in Rancho Esperanza he ruled by his wit and hauteur.

I was always inspired and more than a little amazed by how he could put together a room for practically nothing. On Saturday afternoons he'd take me to estate sales and I'd watch him sort through the detritus of wealthy people's lives, like a treasure hunt in an old, dusty attic: piles of stained damask tablecloths and napkins, silver-plated candlesticks and trifling bibelots amassed over the course of a lifetime. But somehow Bobbie always managed to unearth just the right European linen pillow sham with delicate hemstitching that most people would have overlooked. When everyone was doing their homes in Pierre Deux French provincial or Laura Ashley's cutesy coordinated prints, Bobby was buying trophy heads of antelope and rhinoceros killed by a Rancho Esperanza bwana, suzani fabric pillows, midcentury Mies van der Rohe cane-and-steel chairs, oil portraits of other people's ancestors, or a fine, thread-worn Shiraz carpet he'd pick up for a song and use to cover the ancient linoleum in his laundry room. Bobby Bingham was Ralph Lauren when Ralph Lauren was still Ralph Lifshitz.

Although he lived in a small, rented house—preferring not to deal with ownership and tiresome maintenance—dinner at Bobby's was a coveted invitation. He set his table with old linen the color of crème fraîche, and heavy silver cutlery he'd exhumed on his estate-sale forays. He put out russet Peruvian roses arranged in small Peruvian repoussé silver vases at each place setting. He had china dishes chosen for their individual beauty; no two patterns matched because he said sets reminded him of bridal registries. His tables were inventive and ever changing. But of course, there were always lots of candles because Bobby knew how people looked best and didn't want them to appear any other way.

Not only did Bobby know how to set the stage, he also knew how to cast the dramatis personae. Dinners were a mixture of the most interesting people, some talented, some just beautiful. But no one more beautiful or magnetic than Hadley Stevens. She was already in her sixties when I first met her, but I thought she was just the most exotic woman I'd ever beheld. She was tall and impossibly slender with long, graceful fingers and wide-set reddish-brown eyes. She definitely liked her vodka—always with three olives—smoked cigarettes in a tortoiseshell holder trimmed in gold, and had an impressive vocabulary of four-letter words she never hesitated to use in the most sensual, husky voice. Unlike the careful and self-conscious women I meet today, Hadley had a huge appetite for life, and wasn't afraid to wander the globe like a glutton in search of yet another feast. She'd lived in Europe for a number of years, mostly Spain, but had returned to the States when her mother took ill. During the week she resided in the Hancock Park area of Los Angeles, and on weekends arrived here in her baby blue Mercedes convertible. She was a worldly woman in the best sense and yet during dinner at Bobby's, she would happily sit next to a simple man like Ramón and converse with him in fluent Spanish. Always about horses, which were her passion.

Hadley had had many men, which she spoke about unabashedly. She used to say she got a lot more mileage from her horses than she did from any of her lovers. When I once had the temerity to ask why she had never married, she quipped, "Because I've never found a man who's an easy keeper and behaves on a loose rein." I think Hadley was grateful for Bobby because she hated convention and loved good style. She called him Bing, never Bobby, and was as devoted to him as he to her.

On Saturday nights we'd all go out to dinner, usually at a dive restaurant in the Mexican part of town, or a cheap fish place at the end of the pier where you could get fresh abalone for a few dollars. I'm sure we made an odd quartet: Hadley always so elegant, Ramón with his slicked black hair and cowboy boots, Bobby an old poof, and me just a callow youth still finding his way.

One night we'd decided to splurge and got all dressed up to go to Scandal. We were in one of the red booths by the bar where old Rancho Esperanza preferred to be seated—the unknowing tourists being shunted off to the dining room. We'd just finished our first round of drinks when we saw the maître d' greet a rather dour couple in a familiar yet formal way. They were escorted into the bar and as they passed our table they looked at Ramón as if they couldn't quite believe their eyes. Ramón seemed to shrink in his seat and said hello to them in a cowed manner. Hadley knew the couple—Chicky and Lincoln Crowell—they were Ramón's employers. Hadley had got her black Andalusian from Lincoln and, to defuse the situation, casually mentioned that Ramón had been helping her with Diego on his day off, and she was treating him to dinner. Lincoln couldn't have been more gracious or gentlemanly. He greeted Ramón and told Hadley he'd love to come by her place to see how the horse was doing. His wife never spoke a word.

When the Crowells were seated in a booth safely across the room, Bobby whispered out loud to Hadley, "Madam obviously doesn't approve of you breaking bread with the help."

"Fuck Madam," she replied.

Bumping into them for some reason seemed to put a pall on the rest of the evening. Hadley, who was usually so up and outrageous, drank more than usual and at the end of dinner announced she wanted to have Sunday lunch at Nealey's Tavern.

"Are you sure that's a good idea?" Bobby asked.

"Yes, Bing. I'm quite sure."

The following morning we found ourselves on a winding two-lane road and a quarter of an hour later, we crested the hill and saw the Santa Lucia Valley spread out before us. Where Rancho Esperanza was gaudy bougainvillea on red tile roofs, charming courtyards, and stone terraces, Santa Lucia was wide-open vistas of grassland, chaparral, and oak-studded hills, a muted palette of wheat, sage, and espresso, accented with the rich blackish green of the live oak. Horses and cattle dotted the landscape with an occasional ranch house almost disappearing in the shade of the trees. Except for the narrow paved roads and dusty pickup trucks, there was little to indicate we weren't in the California of two hundred years ago.

Nealey's Tavern, a former stagecoach stop, was a two-story clapboard building, painted white with tall, double-hung windows and a wide, graceful porch that wrapped around three sides. The interior was cool and dim, with very dark—raw umber mixed with black—beadboard wainscoting, and a fire going in the middle of May, but we opted to sit outside under an arbor buzzing with bees and perfumed with the heady scent of honeysuckle. Everyone ordered the house specialty—spicy venison chili—and ice-cold beer. Afterward, we took a walk and stopped in a saddlery, where Hadley bought a pair of paddock boots.

We were already in the car with Hadley behind the wheel when she said she needed coffee before the drive home and headed the car in the opposite direction from which we'd come. Bobby said, "Are you sure you want to do this?"

"Bing," she said to him, "shut up."

She drove for three or four miles and in the near distance, a geographic anomaly—a windmill—appeared. It seemed an illusion, but no, it was really a town of half-timbered homes with gabled roofs—a little Danish village inexplicably plunked down smack in the middle of the Old West.

Hadley chose a pancake house that had a roped-off patio right on the main drag and just as uncharacteristically drank dull, weak coffee for over an hour, hardly speaking. Bobby tried to engage her in conversation, but she was intent on something. He suggested we browse the stores and have a contest to see who could find the ugliest trinket. The Hadley I knew would have jumped up and said, "What fun, Bing. Let's do it!" But she just sat there and watched the passing parade of overweight tourists in Bermuda shorts eating ice cream cones. Then without explanation she got up and said she was ready to go home. She let me drive her baby blue Mercedes while she took a nap in the backseat.

Hadley moved back to Casa de las Flores full-time somewhere around the mid-eighties. She brought with her a girl from Honduras who hardly spoke a word of English. Hadley treated that girl to a life I'm sure she'd never imagined, and even tried to get Fidelia reunited with the child she'd left behind. There was no husband in Fidelia's life, nor did Fidelia want one. I don't think she trusted men and, apparently, did just fine without them. Hadley used to say about her, "Fidelia has more *cojones* than all of the men I've known put together."

Even after Hadley was diagnosed with cancer, she remained a woman with great style, appearing in dramatic turbans and Moroccan djellabas to hide her withering frame. "I don't want a great fuss at my funeral, Bing. Just break out the Cristal and have a hell of a ball." She always said she wanted to be cremated and her ashes scattered in Andalusia, but in the end she decided to be buried with her parents and her sister in the Rancho Esperanza cemetery overlooking the ocean. "If I don't use our family plot, who the hell will? It's not as if some stranger wants to be buried next to Mother. I don't even think my *father* wanted to be buried next to her."

Her bequests were as unpredictable as she: her car went to Bobby, along with a small stipend for taking care of her home

and her dogs. And a quite valuable black chalk drawing by Renoir—
Femme et enfant—was left to Fidelia.

"Why in the world," I asked Bobby, "did she leave her maid a
Renoir? Why didn't she just leave her money?"

"I believe it was symbolic," Bobby said.

"Symbolic of *what*?"

"Do you remember years ago we were eating at Scandal and
bumped into the Crowells, that couple who owned the old Stokes
estate and employed Ramón as their groom?"

I told him I remembered quite well.

"Well, apparently, Lincoln Crowell had been this dashing
flyboy and Hadley had an affair with him when he was already
married to that harridan. Unfortunately, her little indiscretion
resulted in a bigger indiscretion. That was at a time when that
kind of thing was proof you were a slut or a nymphomaniac. Of
course, if you were rich, you found a doctor to handle the situation, and we all know Hadley could have had the situation
handled. But Hadley was always ahead of the pack. She believed
she'd create a perfect child, and she didn't need a husband or
society's permission to do so. She moved to Europe to be with
her sister, Mercedes, and the two of them rented a house in
Andalusia. They were going to raise the baby themselves, and
the child would have two beautiful and exciting mothers. But two
months before the baby was born, Mercedes was killed in an
avalanche while skiing in France. Hadley completely fell apart.
She came back to the States, had the baby, but lost her resolve.
When she came to her senses, it was too late. It was a decision
she regretted for the rest of her life.

"Periodically, when she got really blue or really drunk, poor
Hadley would drive out to the Santa Lucia Valley to look for her
baby. The adoption had been handled through her lawyer, so at
least Hadley had some idea where the baby had gone. She always

thought she'd know that child the minute she saw him. She used to dream of him. I don't know if she actually wanted to meet him, if she was brave enough, but she needed to know what had become of him. That's why she left the Renoir to her maid. Because Hadley admired Fidelia for having the heart and the guts to do what she didn't."

Bobby spent the last five years of his life holed up in Casa de las Flores, clipping coupons and watching the plaster flake off the walls. He liked to say that both he and the house were in a state of romantic collapse. When he overdosed on sleeping pills it took me completely by surprise. The last time I'd seen him he'd seemed fine and had invited me to Casa de las Flores for "cocktails at moonrise." We were on the terrace, taking in the magnificent vista and drinking champagne out of Hadley's Baccarat, when Bobby began a lively rant. But Bobby always went on about people who didn't meet his standards.

"I don't know how you can deal with these New People," he said. "They move here because they think it's beautiful and then they tear down everything of beauty and replace it with their own atrocious taste. You can hardly walk on any street without seeing some monstrous remodel or ersatz Tuscan farmhouse going up. It's an Italian Levittown with twelve-million-dollar tract homes on steroids. There used to be horses in pastures and bridle paths by the side of the road. Now the pastures are gone and the paths are covered in seven inches of asphalt. The cars zoom by so fast you can hardly walk your*self*, much less a horse.

"And that 'All About Town'—that social column or whatever it's supposed to be. I just can't bear it. Who *are* these people he's writing about? The Rancho Esperanza I knew seems to have vanished. The plutocrats have been overtaken by the parvenus. Mrs. Stevens used to fill her Music Pavilion with actual music and elegant people. Now it's just another house, and the only reminder of its glorious past is a tacky little music stand the new owners put in their powder room to use as a towel rack. The Rancho Esperanza Country Club was the finest club in town. These were the people with the education and the manners and the grace to go with their money. The club is now just a bunch of cranky octogenarians. And who'll replace them when they're gone? Certainly not their children.

"That loutish Crawfordtonian—he's the embodiment of everything that has gone wrong with the upper class. Would you ever suspect he comes from American aristocracy? With his bloodlines he should have been a thoroughbred and what did he become? An incurious mule. A born-again buckaroo. Even the Rancho Esperanza Country Club wouldn't want him for a member. No matter what you may think of George and Barbara Bush's desiccated personalities, at least they knew how to carry on a tradition. They tried to pass the torch to their sons and what did Dubya and Jeb Boy do? They let the torch go out. And you think the Bush girls—those teenybopper twins of his—are going to relight it? Once the torch is out, it's out forever."

Poor Bobby. Hadley was dead, Ramón had moved on to greener pastures, and he never again found anyone to love. The world he wanted so much to be a part of was gone. The only small joy he had was living in Hadley's home and dining at Seven Oaks. He would bring an older woman named Delilah who, according to Bobby, had Titian-red hair and once resembled Rita Hayworth. Unfortunately, by the time I finally met her it was less Titian than Benjamin Moore. But in the end she was one of the few people who came to his memorial.

When I drive out to Santa Lucia now, I can't help but think of Bobby and Hadley, and that odd afternoon. So little has changed in the Valley, I sometimes feel as though they should be sitting in the front seat right next to me. Except for the vineyards that now give the landscape a geometric organization and a seasonal distinctiveness, it might still be the Santa Lucia Valley of thirty years ago. Even real estate prices are surprisingly affordable, at least compared with Rancho Esperanza. Although I'm not sure for how long, as it's definitely beginning to attract a more sophisticated element. Some clients have recently asked me to design a home situated in the middle of the most glorious two hundred acres. We've worked together before—restoring a Rudolph Schindler house in Los Angeles and another home in Rancho Esperanza. But now that their last child is off to college, they've decided to take up a new challenge. When they bought the property, there was a 1940s ranch house with diamond windowpanes, and a rather sad and insignificant front porch. The only thing of interest was the barn, which we're turning into a guesthouse. The rest is being built in what might be called Argentine estancia meets Soho Loft. The husband loves it out there and wants to have a vineyard. But his wife, who attends more charity events than anyone I've ever met and whose photo is *always* in the *Rancho Gazette*, is a little afraid Santa Lucia is too isolated. I keep reassuring her they're very lucky to have bought when they did. I tell her this place is just too beautiful to remain a sleepy little valley forever. Just look at Rancho Esperanza, I say. When I first went there, they rolled up the sidewalks at eight-thirty at night and you could throw a bowling ball down Ocean Avenue and not hit a soul. If you just wait, people will discover Santa Lucia, too. With all the vineyards going in, it's only a matter of time before a Chez Panisse or French Laundry opens up. Then everyone will want to move here. And she says, "Fernando, with what we're spending on this fucking house, you'd better be right."

Say what you will about the nouveaux riches being crass destroyers and conspicuous consumers, it's been my experience they're the ones who actually make things happen. Maybe they try a little too hard to impress one another, but then again Mrs. Astor did leave us a lovely home in Newport. Unlike Bobby, I don't fear the tasteless hordes. If they don't have great personal style, then it's my job to provide it. As much as I miss Hadley and Bobby, life goes on. One of these days, New People will even take over the venerable Rancho Esperanza Country Club. I just hope there'll be someone among them who knows those dreadful green drapes with the yellow ball trim just have to go.

Good Stock
Peter Jorgensen

I wait a few days before calling her house. I don't want to have to make conversation with her husband, though we've known each other since childhood. When I saw him at the Fourth of July party we ran out of things to say in five minutes. What does Claire talk to him about? I wonder. "How many fires did you put out today, hon?" What could she have been thinking? Youthful rebellion is one thing, but Claire had it all—beauty, brains, breeding. How could she have thrown it away on Nacho da Silva?

"Hey, man," he'll say, "how you *doin'*? *Great* seeing you the other day."

"Yeah," I'll say, forced to use the same upbeat buddy-speak, "*great* to see you, *too*. Hey, I was calling to see if I could take you and Claire to dinner." *Right.*

"Let me ask the boss. Honey," he'll call into the kitchen or bedroom or laundry, "it's Peter Jorgensen wanting to . . ."

I'll offer to pick them up. "It's on the way." Nacho will answer the door wearing his silk Tommy Bahama camp shirt with the banana leaves—the shirt he saves for "going out." He'll grab the muscle between my neck and shoulder and give me a spasmodic, two-second massage. "Hey, man. How you *doin'*?"

Claire will greet me with a light, sisterly kiss on my cheek, careful not to arouse Nacho's suspicions. After a few pleasantries, she'll turn to lock the front door, but Nacho will grab the keys out of Claire's hand and lock the door himself. It's a territorial gesture meant to show me that in his macho, working-class world, men are the rulers of their homes. And their wives.

We'll walk down their front path and Nacho's eyes will see the patches of straw-colored lawn, the recycling bin he forgot to take in, the garage door that's been patched but not yet painted, the oil-stained cement driveway. Even before we reach my car, he'll resent me for seeing these things, too.

"You sit in front," Claire will say to her husband. "You have longer legs."

"That's okay, you sit in front," he'll say, not meaning it, and he'll open the car door for her. As she slides in he'll realize she looks a little too pretty tonight, she's tried a little too hard. And I'll wonder if Claire has ever told him about us.

"So how do you like your Prius?" he'll say to the back of my head, and until we get to Ocean Avenue we'll talk car. "Fifty mpg. Man," he'll say, pretending to marvel, "leave it to the Japanese. I heard on the news that blind people think the Prius is actually *too* quiet . . ."

"Then why are they driving them?" Claire will say, straight-faced. And we'll laugh, appreciating her effort to break the ice.

At the restaurant he'll assert control again. "You sit here, honey, so Peter and I can both share you." And I'll take it back by ordering a bottle of wine we both know he could never afford. He'll work the conversation around to the summer he was a fire jumper in Montana or that incident with the pregnant woman he rescued with the jaws of life that made front page of the *Rancho*

Gazette. Then he'll turn to Claire for her affirming look and the words of praise he needs to hear, and she will give them to him.

"You playing any tennis these days?" he'll ask me.

"Anytime I can," I'll say.

"Hey, we should play sometime," he'll say, thinking of his killer serve. "We belong to Seven Oaks . . ."

"If you want, we can just play at my house."

"*Cool*," he'll say, wanting to kick my ass all over my court.

All the while Claire will sit between Nacho and me, quietly sipping her wine. She'll look from Nacho to me, from me to Nacho—the lone spectator in a match played entirely for her benefit.

But *she* answers the phone and my heart soars.

"Hello?"

"Hi, Claire."

"Hi . . . is this . . . Peter?"

"Yeah. Am I calling at a good time?"

"Well, actually . . ."

"You sound like you're in the middle of something."

"I just have to get Nacho's car in by nine and I'm not even dressed yet." I imagine her talking to me in her nightgown, the sun coming through the window silhouetting her long legs. "Can I . . ."

"Actually, I was just calling to see if we could get together."

"Oh, we'd love to. But Nacho's in Mexico on a surf trip." *How lucky can I get?*

"Oh, well. Do you want to get together for lunch? Anyway?"

"Today? Today is just . . . bad. I'm running from one stupid thing to another."

"Well," I press, not wanting her to get away, "how 'bout meeting me for a quick drink? Later."

There's a slight hesitation. "Okay. I'll probably need it."

It's the hour of happiness at Teocalli's and the bar is crowded with men who pay too much alimony (they think) and women hoping not to be noticed by the manager of Smitty's. They needn't worry because at this moment all male eyes are focused on a flat screen above the bar that silently replays Roger Federer's win over Rafael Nadal. There's a male chorus of approval as Federer hits a skimming backhand that leaves Nadal midcourt and I'm waiting for the young, pretty blonde from City College (my alma mater!) to return to her hostess station. I spot my Realtor, Steve Farkey, at the bar with the chubby girl from the escrow office, who's "super nice." Although she probably wants to get married and have children before it's too late, I want to tell her she's at the wrong bar in the wrong town—she's fifty pounds heavier than the Rancho Esperanza CC&Rs allow. If only she would move over two barstools, she might find happiness with the manager of Smitty's, but she, like he, is looking for someone she'll never get. Steve is explaining the "pyramiding effect" of the 1031 tax-free exchange, but his attention is not really on the chubby girl or Wimbledon. His radar is sweeping the room looking for a new client, a connection, a name he can one day drop. I avoid catching his eye. Vince Rizzo isn't as lucky. He and his wife, the luscious Miss Philippines, are having dinner with Fred and Freyda Ball—all regulars in the *Rancho Gazette* social column Steve Farkey writes. Sensing an *RG* scoop, Steve slides off his barstool deserting the chubby girl from escrow.

I'm shown to the last booth in the rear of the restaurant, where I can survey the entire room and watch the chubby girl, who doesn't quite know what to do. She swivels on her stool to watch Steve, who hovers over a table she would never be invited to join. I can see he's told the Rizzos and the Balls who I am—"the dot-com guy I sold the Mediterranean house on Jacaranda to." Freyda Ball has to peer over her shoulder to see me. She gives me a look that says, "I'm rich and you're rich and we should know each other." Even from across the room she radiates bad juju. But who cares about any of this. The only reason I'm even here is Claire. How strange life is, I think, how unpredictable. How amazing I will get Claire after all these years, and I *will* get her. I saw it in her face on the Fourth of July—"Rescue me, make me feel young again and desirable." But after twenty minutes and a margarita I worry Claire won't show. I regret not giving her my cell number. I call her home but the machine picks up and I don't leave a message. I worry Nacho has come home early—"The swell never hit"—and she has to deal with him, be the good wife. Or she's been in an accident. Or could she possibly have changed her mind? Was there hesitance in her voice? Then she walks into the restaurant and I can see a look of stress on her face and I want to reassure her that it's going to be okay. Her entire life will all be okay. I wave and when she spots me she breaks into a wide smile and her expression begins to relax. In jeans and a white cotton shirt, she makes all the other women in the room look like they've tried too hard. Vince Rizzo checks the tits and ass as she walks past his table. His wife checks it, too. Freyda Ball fingers her diamond earring, reassuring herself that Claire is too pretty to be smart.

"Sorry," Claire says. "Traffic. There never used to be traffic here."

"I ordered a Damiana margarita," I say, half rising from the table, kissing her on the cheek. "Can I get you one, too?" I can already feel the effects.

"That'd be great." She sits across from me and I signal the waitress and ask her to bring two more. Claire looks over her shoulder and then leans in to me. "My social status has just gone up about a hundred percent sitting here with you."

"What do you mean?"

"That woman at the table over there?" She refers to Freyda Ball. "Our kids are in the same class at Englander. I'm sure she thinks our family is on scholarship because, you know, the name? Da Silva? Mexican? And Nacho being a fire captain? She has no idea my grandmother started the school in the first place. She can hardly bring herself to talk to me, and when she does she's very condescending."

"Well, maybe someone should clue her in," I say.

"Like it would really change her. And that couple they're with, the Rizzos? They live in my old house. It's completely remodeled now. I'm sure they spent a gazillion dollars on it. Mother goes crazy every time someone mentions him or she reads his name."

"The *New* People," I say, imitating Chicky's imperious voice.

"I brought Dad back to the old house a few months ago for an Englander School fund-raiser they were giving. Dad was very upset about the changes they made to the property. You know they sold off the meadow."

"I heard."

"Anyway, he disappeared from the party and apparently walked all the way down to the old stud barn by himself just to see if they had any horses. When he came back from the barn, he was staggering and not able to talk and Nacho realized he was having a stroke and called nine-one-one."

"When I saw him I noticed he was kind of slurring his words."

"And did you see his arms? They're all bruised from the Coumadin. I don't know whether it was the stress of seeing the old place again or what. I probably never should've brought him back there."

"I'm sure it wasn't anything you did. It was just a lifetime of those Fourth of July barbecued ribs and the Welsh rarebit my mother used to make."

Claire touches my hand, abruptly changing the subject. "God, it's funny sitting here with you. Being able to talk to you again. As if we're picking up from yesterday."

I'm finally with Claire. Alone. Or alone as we can be in a restaurant full of people. Whom she hates. Her girls are almost grown and we can move away, we don't have to live here, we can buy any house we want, a separate wing for her girls. Chicky and Lincoln can even come with us. Claire can have horses . . .

Our drinks arrive and we clink glasses in a toast. "Welcome home," she says. We look into each other's eyes, she takes a long sip, and then the tip of her tongue licks the salt crystals from her lips. "My mother-in-law swears by Damiana," she says. "She has a small glass every night before going to bed. It comes in a squat bottle that looks like it was designed by Fernando Botero. But supposedly it's a pregnant woman modeled after the Incan god of fertility. Rosa says Damiana is the reason she and Manny are still *romantico*."

Rosa and Manny. Pirata and Alfonso. The John Deere and her perfect cupcake breasts. I wonder what they look like now. "So they still manage to get it on with the help of Saint Damiana."

"I don't think Manny and Rosa ever had any problems in that department."

"Evidently not. They had five children."

"I know, and I have no idea when they found the time or energy or privacy. My parents couldn't even do it in a huge house with just me."

"How do you know they didn't do it?"

"Oh, the twin beds were a hint. I mean, if you really like each other, who has twin beds? I think my mother is kind of chilly—"

"Kind of?" *She's a bitch is what she is.*

"—and my father was . . . 'a trifler' as mother would say about those kinds of men. I don't think my mother knew. But she probably suspected."

"Lincoln a trifler? So whom did he trifle with?" *Who wouldn't want a little trifle being married to Chicky?*

"Hadley Stevens?" she says, wondering if I know the name.

"How do you know?"

"I saw them once. In the stud barn. When I was about eight."

"You *caught* him? You caught your father being a stud in the barn?"

"I know," she says, rolling her eyes. "Although I wasn't quite sure what was going on. I just knew, instinctively, it wasn't something you barge in on."

"I always thought she was kind of sexy, Hadley Stevens."

"So you remember her?"

"She rode around on that Andalusian named Diego and smoked with a cigarette holder. And she had that voice like Lauren Bacall. Right?"

"That *was* Hadley," she says with a tinge of sarcasm.

"How could you *not* remember her? We were never officially introduced but at one of those Fourth of July parties she wanted me to help her put this kite in the air. It was a huge red, white, and blue box kite with tails about five feet long. We went running down by the pond and scared away all the swans and she was laughing and when I finally got it in the air I was all sweaty and I handed her the string and she said to me, 'My, you really know how to get a girl hot.'"

"She *said* that? She *flirted* with you?"

"It was no big deal. She flew the kite for about two minutes, got bored, and gave it back. That was my big moment with Hadley Stevens. So what did your father say after you caught him?"

"Nothing. They were preoccupied. I'm not sure if they even saw me."

"What was the upshot?"

"I didn't stay for the finale."

"You know what I mean."

"I never mentioned it to him and he never mentioned it to me. I mean, what are you supposed to say?"

"Is that why you were so sexually precocious?"

"I wasn't sexually precocious," she says, smacking my arm playfully. "God. That makes me sound like I was really out there. Maybe you were just sexually *backward*."

"No doubt. But hey, that's probably because my mother wasn't fucking the neighbor right in front of me. She was very square that way."

"Well," she says, taking my hand in hers, giving it a slight squeeze, "that's probably why you turned out so sweet." Her eyes are starting to get a little glazed.

"Don't call me sweet," I say, intertwining our fingers. *I'm touching her.* "Men don't like to be called sweet."

"Why not?"

"It sounds weak."

"Maybe that's why you turned out so virile and masculine and successful and competent and intelligent . . . and sexy."

"That'll work."

She smiles, our hands come apart, and she leans back against the booth. "So. Did it feel funny coming to the party when it wasn't at the old house?"

"Your parents used to make it into such a big deal. And I'd have to help set them up every year . . . dragging those hay bales out of the barn. But I still think about those parties. They made an impression."

"I know. I still think about them, too."

"My Realtor, Steve Farkey, who's at the bar, told me the old stud barn was turned into a screening room that was on the cover of *Architectural Digest*."

"They also turned my old nursery into their high colonic room."

"You're kidding. What's *that*?"

"Like it sounds. I saw it when I went there for that Englander School fund-raiser. They were very matter-of-fact about it. They do in-home high colonics and have a colonicist? Is that what you'd call her? Who comes over and does the—whatever they do. And the whole contraption is designed to look like a brass antique espresso machine. Nacho calls it a crapacinno."

"I can just imagine your mother's reaction. I just hope they took down your Babar wallpaper."

"Of course. Poor Babar wouldn't want to see that. I can't believe you remember these things," she says.

"I remember everything about that house. I even remember how many of those antique dog plates your mother had hanging over the sideboard in the dining room." *Way before I'd ever heard of Sèvres porcelain.*

"How many?"

"Fifteen. Five on the bottom, four, three, two, one."

"Jesus. Even *I* don't remember how many dishes there were. You must have been looking very hard."

"That house was like a habitat where some exotic species lived. I guess I thought it would tell me something."

"About?"

"What it was like to be the Crowells of Rancho Esperanza."

"It wasn't that great," she says flatly. Then she perks up with polite good cheer. "But look what happened to *you*. Look what *you've* accomplished. We're all so *proud* of you." She takes the plastic straw out of her drink and begins to bend it around her finger, first one way and then the other. "It was a funny town to be brought up in, don't you think? It was so insular. But it's changed a lot since you were here. Even the raft in front of our old cabana is gone. They took it out of the water about ten years ago because of liability. The only thing still left is Smitty's. That's in a time warp. Remember that kooky store on Ocean Avenue that sold shells? 'There are so *many* things you can do with shells.' And that kind of English-looking shop that had 'clothes for the country lady and gent.' And that little French restaurant with the lace curtains? And Scandal where my parents sat in the same booth year after year? It's all real estate and escrow offices now."

"I remember when your Princeton boyfriend took you to that French restaurant for your birthday. I thought he must really be loaded to afford to take you to a French restaurant."

"That's so . . . pathetic."

"No kidding."

"Chez Pierre. It was such a hokey restaurant where they served coquille St. Jacques. When was the last time you saw *that* on a menu? And the ladies' room had wallpaper of pink French poodles sitting at dressing tables and looking in hand mirrors. And Chuck—he was *such* a stiff. He's probably some banker now like his father, living in Greenwich, Connecticut."

"But he was Princeton. I was City College. I didn't even know what a banker was."

"You were about a hundred times smarter than he was."

"And sweeter?"

"Oh. Definitely sweeter." She leans forward again, elbows on the table. "So what made you decide to come back? I remember you saying you couldn't wait to leave. Now you live next door to Ollie Shawl. I can't believe you bought a house next to Ollie."

"Why?"

"He was the one who called my father and told him we were making out on the balcony of the cabana."

"That was Ollie?"

"He was my father's lawyer. And Hadley's lawyer. He represented all the old guard in town and knew everything that was going on in everybody's lives."

"The look on your father's face when he came downstairs and saw us. 'What kind of a crum-bum are you?' So perfectly Lincoln. But of course, I was trying to have sex with his daughter. I guess, in retrospect, 'crum-bum' actually shows . . . restraint. What did he say to you? In the car? On the way home?"

"He didn't say anything. He said we were never going to tell my mother or talk about it again."

"You and your father have kind of an understanding in that department, don't you? I thought she was the one who made sure you got sent away to school."

"No. It was my father."

"That's funny . . . I always thought your father liked me. I was polite. I knew what fork to use. Your mother . . . she was the scary one."

"My mother used to have all these absurd rules about what was proper and what wasn't. 'Nice girls don't walk home from the beach in a wet bathing suit with a damp, sandy towel wrapped around their waist. Nice girls don't wear bikinis and lie in the sun greased up with Bain de Soleil. Nice girls don't wear frosted nail polish or have their ears pierced. Mexican *babies* have their ears pierced.' It wasn't until I went away to school and met other people who came from Good Families and saw them wearing bikinis and Bain de Soleil and snorting heroin that I realized all of her ideas about life were completely wacko. But she's mellowing," Claire says with a shrug. "So what are you going to do now that you're back here?"

"That depends a lot on you, actually."

"How so?"

"I came back because I can't quit thinking about you."

"Wow," she says in a way that's impossible to read.

"Are you surprised?"

"No. I'm relieved." She takes my hand and turns it palm-side up as if she's about to tell my fortune. "Because I think about you, too. There're some days when it seems you're all I think about."

"So." *Come home with me now. Let me make love to you.* "How could you have married Nacho? What could you have been thinking, Claire? When I saw you two together . . . it just doesn't make any sense."

"It doesn't? Really? It's so obvious. He was forbidden fruit, like you. Only darker. And foreign. And he was good in bed. He excited me. They wouldn't let me have you so I picked the most inappropriate person I could find. My father, to this day, can't forgive Nacho. And Nacho can't stand my father. And poor Chicky. I really rocked her little world, didn't I?" She lets go of my hand. "If I could? I'd get as far away from Rancho Esperanza as it's possible to get." She looks at me with those bright blue eyes, knowing exactly what I'm going to say.

"Then let me take you away. Anywhere you want."

"Yes. That would really do it. That would give my father another stroke for sure."

"I've had lots of time to think about this. I know this is the right thing."

"I've got kids. I'm not eighteen anymore. I have responsibilities."

"I understand. I would never ask you to hurt them in any way. But they must see you're not happy."

"They love their father."

"I'm sure they do."

"They have no idea what a bastard he is."

"So what are we going to do?"

"Nothing."

"I don't believe that. I don't believe that's what you really want."

"What I want is so completely irrelevant."

"You made a mistake. It doesn't mean you can't undo it. You're a grown woman now. Take control."

"I tried to. Once. When I came back home after college. I even got your phone number from your mother. I got your number and where you lived and I told my parents I was going to drive to San Francisco and surprise you."

"And?"

She leans back in the booth and folds her arms across her chest. "And my father said to me, 'Before you go I want you to talk to Ollie Shawl.'"

"What did he want Ollie to do? Make out a prenup or something?"

"We could never get married. I should have nothing to do with you. For my own good. That's what Ollie told me."

"*What?* Why?" After all these years, I'm still outraged at the injustice. The insult. Like a fifteen-year-old who has just been called a crum-bum. Or told to put the picnic baskets in the trunk of the car. Or been referred to, once again, as *the cook's boy*. "Because I didn't come from Good Stock?"

"Why don't you get it?"

"What's to get?"

"Go talk to Ollie Shawl." Her blue eyes are blinking rapidly. "You live right next *door* to him, for god's sake."

"What are you talking about?" I say to her.

"Hadley and my father?"

"So? Big deal. You think your father is the only man who's ever *trifled*?"

"My father *is* your father," she says, like I'm the most obtuse person she's ever had the misfortune to deal with.

"Lincoln?"

"Ta da!" she says, a magician who has just pulled the rabbit out of the hat. "Get it now?" Her arms are like the scales of Justice, perfectly balanced. But then they tilt. "I shouldn't be the one even telling you all this," she says almost petulantly. "But it's so *typical*, isn't it? Everything has to be polite. Everything has to be kept quiet. Everything has to be done to protect my mother from knowing. And my father from being found out. And Hadley, even though she's *dead*. I don't know *why* you had to come back. I was doing *fine* before you came here. We were *all* doing fine. What is it you *want* from us?"

I feel a wave of nausea. I don't know if it's because I'm drunk, or that Claire has just informed me my entire life has been one big mind fuck.

"Excuse me," I say. I stand up and the room begins to dim. There's a roaring in my head and I hope I can make it to the bathroom before I pass out.

The room is swirling and as I stand at the toilet I put my hand on the cool wall to steady myself. I want the margarita out of my bloodstream and think, in my drunken stupor, that maybe I can just piss it out and I'll be sober and clear-thinking. But it doesn't work. I go to the sink and splash cold water on my face. When I pull a towel out of the dispenser, I notice the black-and-white framed photograph on the wall. It's from an old edition of "All About Town." The headline reads SINGING SENSATION MARIO LANZA COMES TO RANCHO ESPERANZA. Someone has planted a kiss on the glass. To delay exiting the bathroom for just a few more seconds, I stand back to examine the photo. Four beautiful young women dressed in gowns, each holding a tray of cocktails. *Her servants off doing their part for the war effort*, the text reads, *Mrs. Stevens recruited daughters Hadley and Mercedes, along with friends*

Chicky Stokes and Delilah Porter, to pass out splendid refreshments. The greasy imprint of full lips veils my mother's face. I turn around and vomit violently into the toilet.

When I get back to the booth, the waitress is depositing a menu and a new basket of chips on the table. "The woman who was here told me to tell you she had to leave. Do you want to order dinner? We have a few specials I can tell you about."

Three months have passed since that evening. I've never heard from Claire again. And I'm way beyond caring. Nor has Lincoln called to welcome me into the family—"Cat's out of the bag, M' Boy." Even Ollie and Danzy Shawl now turn the other way to avoid seeing me when our cars pass on Jacaranda Drive. It's a small town and sooner or later I know I'll come face-to-face with one of them. But I'll pretend that nothing has ever happened. Like the good Crowell I am.

It's my mother I think about now. Not the beautiful one with the husky laugh, but the one who hardly laughed at all. The one who worked as a cook in the Crowell house. The pretty young widow who once said to her son as she smoothed back my hair, "It will be the best thing for you, being around people who have money. At least you'll get to see another way of life. And maybe you'll learn some things from them that I could never teach you."

ALL ABOUT TOWN
By Steve Farkey

Friday the 13th. Who among us doesn't feel just a *little* superstitious? Maybe you don't fly on that day. Or you put off having surgery. Why take the chance? I don't believe in superstitions myself, but Friday, October 13, 2006 will be remembered as perhaps the unluckiest day in Rancho Esperanza's long and magnificent history.

Our usual perfect coastal weather has given way to Santa Ana conditions, and the only place to cool off is at one of our many beautiful beaches. Rancho Esperanza's fire chief Ignacio da Silva—known *all about town* as Nacho "the singing fireman"—issues a Red Flag Alert. "At noon the temperature had already hit 98 with the humidity at only 9 percent," he tells me. "The long summer drought had made the brush extremely dry. It was the ideal condition for a wildfire."

As anyone who lives in Rancho Esperanza knows, our community is no stranger to wildfires. The 1965 Fox Canyon fire consumed 1,500-plus acres and damaged over forty dwellings before it was brought under control. And in 1987, the Dominguez ridge fire jumped Old Coast Highway and burned all the way to the Pacific Ocean, destroying a 173 homes. "We definitely have a fire season," Nacho tells me. "It's almost as if

Paradise has to have a reality check every once in a while."

As chance would have it, Nacho's brother, Alfonso, calls in the fire. At about 2:00 pm Alfonso, a gardener on the old Casa de las Flores estate—a captivating knoll-top Italianate villa built in 1907 by the vivacious and beautiful "Queen of Rancho Esperanza Society" Lillian Stevens, and currently owned by Cheryl and Elliot Kornblatt—notices something very unusual. "I saw a bright light shining on the compost heap, like from a magnifying glass, and then I saw smoke," Alfonso recalls. "By the time I got there, it was already on fire. I grabbed a rake to smother it but the wind had come up. I could see sparks being blown everywhere. I put the fire out in the compost heap, but the sparks had started another fire by the side of the road."

At 2:10 the call comes in: a small brush fire north of Star Pine Hill. Two county fire engines respond. By the time Nacho and his men get to the scene, the wind has kicked up to twenty miles an hour and the entire hillside is engulfed in flames. As the fire races up the mountain consuming sagebrush and tinder-dry chaparral, Nacho requests a second alarm. More fire trucks arrive, but fanned by the winds, the fire is already changing direction, jumping across the tree-lined street and threatening adjacent houses—some of them in the multi-million dollar range. "We quickly realized we had a situation on our hands," Nacho says.

Danzy Shawl, president of the Gardening Club, is standing under the rose-covered arbor on the grounds of her enchanting Moorish Mediterranean, Casa Esmeralda, designed by famed Palm Beach architect Addison Mizner. "It was dry as a bone and pretty windy and I could see my roses just wilting in the heat. I was giving them extra water when I smelled the smoke. Then I heard the fire engines racing up Jacaranda Drive and I said to my husband, Ollie, 'There's a fire up the street. I hope it isn't a bad one.'"

Peter Jorgensen, the dot-com billionaire who just last month tied the knot with Leigh McHugh (whose late husband, Mac McHugh, created MJM Electronics), is about to fly off in their private jet to visit Peter's mother on the Oregon Coast. "We had just taken off and were flying over Rancho Esperanza when we saw the fire from the air," their pilot tells me. Leigh adds, "There was a strong wind and we knew it could be bad. We decided we should turn around and land. We tried to drive home but by the time we reached the bottom of Jacaranda Drive and Vista del Mar, the fire department was telling residents to evacuate."

> ## "We quickly realized we had a situation on our hands."
> —Fire Chief Ignacio da Silva

By 5:00 pm the wind we all know as "sundowners" is gusting 50 to 70 miles an hour and the fire is declared out of control. Air tankers have been summoned to try to stop the fire's downhill run. "We knew if it jumped Vista del Mar we were in big trouble," Nacho says. "If it did that, there was a real good chance it wouldn't stop until it hit the Pacific."

At Seven Oaks, Chicky and Lincoln Crowell—who some might remember used to raise those beautiful Andalusian horses—begin to load their more valuable possessions into their cars. "You'd think that living on a golf course you have a green barrier to protect you," Lincoln declares. "But I've lived here long enough to know that fires are mighty unpredictable. They can jump right over one house and land on another." He is right. By 9:00 pm, five homes in Seven Oaks have been engulfed in flames. Including the Crowells' contemporary hacienda-style casita on Clubhouse Drive. The irony? Their son-in-law is Nacho da Silva. "You just feel so bad when you realize you can't save every house," the fire chief says. "The Crowells will be living with my parents in Santa Lucia until they're able to return here."

At 9:15 pm Jerry Green, who owns the dapper men's clothing store Maxwell & Company, watches his 1927 California craftsman-style cottage on Primrose Lane literally implode, sending huge fireballs up in the air only to be carried downhill by the wind. Although he's taken the precaution of spraying his shake roof with foam fire retardant, the heat of the fire is just too much. "It was my worst nightmare," Jerry recalls. "The only thing we were able to save were some photos, a string of pearls, and an old Navajo rug we bought on our honeymoon." He adds philosophically, "We lost almost everything, but then they're only possessions."

Just across the creek, Sally and Walter Topping, who started the Rancho Esperanza Savings and Loan, feel like the luckiest people alive. Their beautiful four-bedroom French Country home dating from 1939 has been spared. Even the mature oaks and olive trees escaped the ravage. "The firefighters were unbelievable," Sally tells me. Walter adds, "They busted their chops saving our house and they're my heroes."

The Englander School is declared an emergency shelter. But rather then swelter inside with no air conditioning or electricity, hundreds of families set their Red Cross cots under the ancient oak trees. With the hills ablaze all around them, they gather in front of the Ball Theater where a TV, powered by generator, has been set up. Everyone is watching for news of their homes. "It was completely eerie," Arnold Ornstein says. "It's like we were watching the fire in visual stereo."

Over 1,200 firefighters, coming from as far away as Idaho and Oregon, are now battling the blaze. All night long choppers can be heard dropping their loads of fire retardant.

For the next 24 hours white ashes fall from the sky like summer snow, covering cars and patio furniture and turning turquoise swimming pools into gray soup.

On the morning of Sunday, October 15th the fire has been declared under control. Over two hundred residences have burned to the ground. The popular eateries Arpeggio and Teocalli's are gone.

Some were luckier than others but it seems everyone has a story to tell:

Arturo Rios, the maitre d' at the Rancho Esperanza Country Club since 1985, fills up garbage pails with water and cleverly thinks to take down the curtains from the club's cozy library. "The water pressure was very low due to the fire. So for two days and nights I put out the hot spots with those wet curtains. They're ruined now but at least the club is still standing." Bravo, Arturo!

Howard and Nancy Berry live in the charming stone house known as the Music Pavilion, originally built by Mrs. Lillian Stevens as a place to entertain the great and the near great on her Casa de las Flores estate. Mario Lanza once sang for Charles Lindbergh in her famous Music Pavilion. Fortunately, the house sustained minimal damage and the Berrys' museum-quality collection of French impressionist drawings, by masters such as Matisse, was unharmed. "You can't believe how relieved we are," Howard says. "We've always loved French 18th and 19th century drawings and we felt phenomenally lucky to have stumbled across these. They were originally displayed in the drawing room of Casa de las Flores." His wife, Nancy, adds, "They're not only priceless but, in a sense, a priceless piece of Rancho Esperanza's history."

Lailani and Vince Rizzo—she is known *all about town* for her stylish parties and Vince is one of Hollywood's most successful producers—watch the fire from the stone terrace of their magnificent twenty-acre home, La Casa al Loma. "We were never in danger," Vince tells me, "but it was an awesome thing to see. It was like sitting through one of my own movies, only this was real!"

Fred and Freyda Ball have taken a break from their philanthropic work and are vacationing in Italy, when Nancy Berry telephones to tell them their home has survived. "We're moving to Santa Lucia to start a vineyard," Freyda tells me, "and our Rancho Esperanza home, which was done by Fernando Laguna, will be on the market. Fred and I have decided to sell the house completely furnished, dishes and all, so someone who lost their home will be able to move right in and get on with their lives."

When Leigh and Peter Jorgensen are finally allowed to return home, they drive up their cypress-lined drive not knowing what to expect. But their secluded and romantic Mediterranean estate and their terraced garden, overflowing with lavender and rosemary, has been spared. They now have three generations of one family living with them. "Our housekeeper, Fidelia, has moved into the guest house with her daughter and granddaughter," Peter tells me. "Leigh and I don't have any children of our own so for us, it's like having a big, happy family."

Miraculously, there is only one

fatality. Rancho Esperanza native, Delilah Porter, was out bird watching in the mountains that afternoon. "When the fire hit," Nacho reports, "it just moved too fast for her to outrun." She is 71 years old and has no immediate family.

Today as my partner, Rámon, and I drive around, we see entire streets where houses used to be, but now they are just chimneys, gravestones marking what used to be Rancho Esperanza's golden rectangle. As a Realtor at Country Town Properties for over twenty years, I've sold so many of these beautiful homes to people who have since become friends. For me, it is a very personal loss.

And the cause of all this devastation, that bright light Alfonso da Silva saw on the compost heap on Friday the 13th? It was determined by the authorities that it was the sun shining through a window of Casa de las Flores, and hitting a vanity mirror sitting on a dressing table. The Kornblatts were in Martha's Vineyard at the time of the fire and could not be reached for comment. "It was no one's fault," Nacho tells me, "a one in a million thing. Almost an act of God. My wife, Claire, and I extend our prayers to the entire community."

Acknowledgments

I would like to thank Jules Weinseider, Howard Kosh, Ana Rodriquez, Marcie Feldman, Shirley Ann Hurley, and Micholyn Brown for their inspiration. Thanks to Allan Langdale for adding his wit to my prose and for getting into character, and to the other good sports who agreed to pose: Ellen Easton, Sharon Fisher, Dallas Steele, Jules Weinseider, Howard Kosh, Mindy Marin, Gabe Rotter, and Ana Rodriquez. Thanks to Oliver Tollison for the cover photo, Nancy Englander for looking so elegant atop Aladdin, and to Virginia Castagnola-Hunter for the use of her beautiful garden and home.

Thank you to Chris Carter, always my first reader. Thanks to my agent, Lane Zachary, always my second reader. Thanks to my editors at Other Press, Corinna Barsan and Yvonne Cárdenas, who saw things I never would have. Special thanks to Judith Gurewich, who championed the book.

Thanks to my lawyers, David Weiner and Nancy Boxwell, who look out for me.

And thanks to my dear friends, Ann and Curt Massie, Adele and Rick Carter, Kimberly Carter Gamble and Foster Gamble, Sonia Scheideman, Gabe Rotter, Steve and Tamara Stafford, Ruthie Carter Kosh, Carol Montgomery, Patrick and Michele Soon-Shiong. You were there when it counted. Thank you forever.